**"GET READY, PARTNER,"
THE WALKIE-TALKIE CRACKLED.
"CREWS AND HIS BROTHER ARE
ON THEIR WAY UP, LOADED
AND DANGEROUS."**

"If they so much as lift an armpit," barked Tiny fiercely, "I'll blow 'em to heaven and let 'em drop down to hell!"

Seconds ticked by. Behind the closed door, Tiny finally heard footsteps along the carpeted hallway. Someone halted outside. There was the sound of objects falling and then rapid footsteps.

Tiny's first reaction was to fling open the door, but years of experience warned him not to. Then, in a split second, the door dissolved into yellow flames and exploding shrapnel.

"THE BOUNTY HUNTER is fast-moving, sexy, humorous, and very well written....
A book you can't put down once you start it."

Rosemary Rogers

Also by
Tiny Boyles and Hank Nuwer

THE DEADLIEST PROFESSION

THE BOUNTY HUNTER

BY TINY BOYLES
AND HANK NUWER

#2 A KILLING TRADE

PLAYBOY
PAPERBACKS

THE BOUNTY HUNTER: A KILLING TRADE

Copyright © 1981 by William Boyles and Hank Nuwer

Cover photograph by Ron Mesaros originally appeared in *OUI* magazine: copyright © 1979 and 1981 by Playboy Publications, Inc.

Published simultaneously in the United States and Canada by Playboy Paperbacks, New York, New York. Printed in the United States of America. Library of Congress Catalog Card Number: 81-81398. First edition.

Books are available at quantity discounts for promotional and industrial use. For further information, write to Premium Sales, Playboy Paperbacks, 1633 Broadway, New York, New York 10019.

ISBN: 0-872-16902-2

First printing September 1981.

Dedication

Tiny: For Lacy J. Dalton, brothers, sisters, and kin.
Hank: For my son Christian, friends, family,
and road acquaintances.

Acknowledgments

To Alexis, Cathy, Deb, and Rosemary for support and help rendered.

All characters and events are fictitious, even though some of this material gives us the sweats all over.

Chapter One

While America celebrated Thanksgiving with festive turkey dinners, Tiny Ryder was scarfing down greasy hamburgers at a Las Vegas truck stop. He was after a far different bird from the kind our forefathers feasted upon. The turkey he was tracking was a shiftless armed robber named Jock Crews who had run out on a $50,000 bond that bail bondsman Joey Hudson—Tiny's boss—had posted. From his Sunset Strip office in Hollywood, Joey had sent his six foot six, 389-pound hunter of men after Crews after learning that an all-points bulletin had been issued on the skip-out in Denver, Colorado. The new charge was murder in the first degree. Police wanted Crews for questioning in the cold-blooded stabbing death of his own daughter.

"Well, partner," Tiny mumbled through a mouthful of bun and beef that passed through a furnace-door-sized slit in the middle of a chest-length black beard. "This sure is a hell of a comedown from the Thanksgiving we enjoyed last year."

The mass of gristle and muscle whom Tiny was addressing nodded his head in solemn agreement. Not that the bounty hunter expected a verbal reply from his right-hand man, who went simply by the handle of Hammer. The bounty hunter liked to joke that the Good Lord had allowed Hammer 1,000 words to utter in his entire lifetime, and the quiet man still had

999 left. If silence was golden, the thirty-two-year-old lockjawed silent partner would one day be a billionaire.

Tiny, on the other hand, could outjabber an angry magpie. And since he stood about as tall and wide as a Sherman tank, there weren't many men brave or foolish enough to interrupt him when he talked.

"Sure am hungry," Tiny said to Hammer. "Of course, I've always been a light eater."

Hammer raised an eyebrow in disbelief.

"Yep." Tiny guffawed. "As soon as it's light out, I start to eat."

Tiny flashed his hand to a waitress and signaled for four more burgers and a pitcher of iced tea. "Boy, I'd give anything for some nice turkey breast—or any other kind of breast for that matter." The big man chuckled. "Last Turkeyday, as I recall, we enjoyed four different dinners."

Hammer left his fork in an impaled baked potato and flashed his open hand in disagreement.

"What's that?" asked Tiny, long accustomed to reading his partner's sign language. "Oh, yeah, you're right. We had *five* dinners. Damn! That's even worse. I sure hate wasting a Thanksgiving flitting along the road like this. Ain't no easier pickup in the world than to bogart on in while a skip is chowing down his turkey dinner with his kin. I don't care how much a crook tries to ignore his family; there's just something that sends a man back home on Thanksgiving."

Hammer nodded agreement, pushing back his blue L. L. Bean watchcap on his ample forehead and then sliding back from the table to signify that he'd eaten enough.

"Of course, we're not hard to get along with on Thanksgiving, are we, Hammer?"

Again, a nod of agreement.

"We let every one of them five skips finish his meal. Even allowed 'em seconds of pumpkin pie. And in honor of the holiday, we didn't put cuffs on any of them, either, so's their families wouldn't feel bad."

Hammer creased his forehead and shook his head from left to right.

"What's that? Oh, yeah. We did have to cuff that one old boy from Gardena, but that was just 'cause you caught him stuffing a carving knife under his shirt."

A bosomy redhaired waitress sashayed up to the table and dropped a large paper sack in front of Tiny. "There you are, hon, two whole chickens raw and a sack of steak bones to go. That's the damnedest doggie bag I ever seen."

Tiny peeled off a twenty-dollar bill and tucked it into her apron top. "It ain't for my dog, darling," he rasped. "We got a hungry wolf waitin' on us."

Once outside, Tiny inhaled the desert air with satisfaction. It would be nice to take in a casino or two, he reflected, but Las Vegas wasn't going anywhere and he was: to northern Colorado, by midnight, to be exact.

Walking across the asphalt parking lot to the motor home, Tiny and Hammer looked curiously at a beefy man in a silver Porsche jacket who motioned them over. The two partners exchanged a shrug and approached diffidently.

"Yeah?" growled Tiny, who didn't like the man on sight. The guy had an oily quality about him. "Just like the gunk you get in your comb," the bounty hunter would later remark to Hammer.

Silver Jacket gave both men an oozing smile and pointed to a pickup truck with a Chinook camper in back. "Got just what you lonely gentlemen need in a lonely town like this."

"Oh yeah, what?" the bounty hunter asked, motivated by curiosity.

The oily man grasped Tiny by the elbow and led him to the back of the camper. Tiny jerked back his arm as if repelled by the touch, but Silver Jacket gave no sign that he had noticed. Looking carefully around to make certain that no one else was in sight, he opened the camper door with a jolt. "Welcome to Lollipop heaven!"

Tiny and Hammer peered inside, noting a scent of something unpleasant coming from within. Propped up on gaudy, filthy, imitation satin sheets was a flat-chested nude girl who was blinking uncomfortably in the sudden light. Tiny took a deep breath and turned to Hammer.

"You take this bag and feed our wolf," he commanded his partner. "He'll want a bit of exercise afterwards."

The quiet man nodded solemnly and moved stolidly away to carry out his orders. Tiny turned to Silver Jacket, who held his palm out expectantly.

"I never lay down my money until I'm first sure of the merchandise," said the bounty hunter, his tone quiet yet all the more menacing for that.

Grasping both sides of the entranceway to haul himself up, Tiny passed with difficulty into the Chinook. After closing the camper door in the oily man's face, he addressed himself to the girl. "Got any light in here?"

Obediently, the prostitute moved toward a small battery-powered portable affair and flicked on the switch. Even in the pale yellow light, Tiny managed to get a good look at her frail, white body. Brown and purple bruises covered every limb, and one nipple was clearly infected.

"How old are you, darling?" asked Tiny with a catch in his voice.

The girl had been asked the question before. "Eighteen," she cooed in a voice obviously meant to be seductive, and her right hand curled about her unhurt breast.

"No, don't do that," Tiny said, tossing a blanket at her. "I just want to talk."

"Oh," the girl answered knowingly, "you're one of *those*. Well, then, I want to suck your hard cock, suck it until all the juices come out. . . ."

"That's enough." Tiny irritably interrupted the recitation. "I want to talk about *you*."

Instinctively, the girl shot a frightened look toward the door. "Don't worry," Tiny told her, hauling out a .357 from a shoulder holster obscured by his black leather vest. "Ain't no way he's coming in here to hurt you. Now, let's start over again. How old *are* you?"

The girl closed her eyes painfully. "Fourteen," she whispered.

Tiny felt the meal he'd just eaten turn over in his stomach. "Christ!" he ejaculated. "What's your real name? Where are you from?"

"Debbie Vaughn, from Fayetteville, Arkansas. I've been here in Vegas with *him*," she spat angrily, "for three months. I'd run away, trying to go to L.A., and this here's where my money run out. He and a couple other men found me and treated me real nice for a week or so. Then . . . then"—she shuddered—"everything changed."

"Go on," Tiny said gently. He took a corner of one soiled sheet and gently dabbed at the girl's face. A film of greasy makeup came off in his hand, instantly transforming her from woman to little girl.

"One night, he—his name is Al—dragged me into the living room and blindfolded me. The other men were there, too, and someone I'd never met, who had an accent I'd heard someplace before. He had some kind of strange animal with him, too. Every so often I would hear it growl or crunch on some bones."

"Did you catch this new guy's name?"

"No, but they were all afraid of him and very respectful."

"What happened that night?"

"They undressed me real rough. Al had bought me a red dress that I loved, and someone tore it down the middle, right off of me. A knife scraped across my chest and slit apart my bra. They threw me down and tied my hands to my legs. Then all of them took a turn with me, first the leader, then the others."

"Did they hurt you?"

"Yes, especially the leader. I guess Al had told him I was a virgin, but he had never bothered to ask me. (I had had a sixteen-year-old boyfriend when I was in the eighth grade.) Anyway, when no blood came out, the guy was furious. He slapped me, kicked me, did things to me you wouldn't want done to a dog. They pinned a clothespin to my nipple here and took turns twisting it."

"All right," Tiny interrupted. "I get the idea. Do you want to go home?"

Debbie looked at Tiny with amazement, as if that possibility had never occurred to her. "How?"

Tiny pulled out his biker wallet, popping open the silver snaps on either side of the Harley-Davidson eagle. He pulled out three crisp Ben Franklin bills and lay them in front of her. "That should get you some new clothes, a phone call home, and a plane ticket," he said.

The girl's eyes welled with tears, but before she could reply, the Chinook camper suddenly surged forward. Tiny grabbed his .357 and reached for the door handle.

"He's taking off," Tiny shouted. "Jump, Debbie!"

The big man leaped through the narrow entranceway, catching one black boot as he did so, slamming shoulder first into the pavement. His whole left side afire, Tiny turned to catch sight of the young girl standing nude in the entrance, her face distorted with fear. The pickup, with Al behind the wheel, left the truck stop at forty and sped down a sideroad toward the interstate.

A Nevada Highway Patrol officer who had just

pulled into the rest stop for coffee immediately gunned his vehicle in determined pursuit.

"Get that sucker," Tiny muttered, jogging painfully toward the Chinook. "Get him."

The powerful patrol car roared to within twenty feet of the Chinook just as the panic-stricken girl leaped out the door, Tiny's three hundred-dollar bills clutched in one hand. When she hit the ground, the patrol car couldn't avoid slamming into her. The impact sent Debbie's body soaring 150 feet through the air. Abandoning the chase, the officer raced outside to where Tiny was painfully striding toward the pile of crumpled flesh. The two arrived simultaneously, finding exactly what they feared they would find.

Chapter Two

"Foster Foster!" cried the voice of a sweet young thing. "If I want your hand in my bra, I'll put it there myself."

A dozen heads in the Kansas City, Missouri, theater turned away from the movie to catch sight of a sandy-haired man wrenching his hand from the thin tank top it had snuggled inside a moment before.

"Shit!" Foster answered, growing red-faced under his spectacles. "What did you have to say it so loud for? Everyone in the place heard you, Sissy."

"I *wanted* them to hear me." Sissy grinned, straightening the garment so that her breasts once again strained enticingly against the red cotton. "It's the only way I can get you to behave. Honestly, Foster! For a professional writer, you sure don't have much couth."

"I was just feeling a little horny."

"A *little* horny? Foster! I swear, you must've been born with too many hormones. All you want to do all day is write and fuck."

"That's not true. I like to eat, too."

"Eat what? Oh, no! I had to ask," she complained, noting the leering expression on Foster's mug.

"I just want to please you," Foster told her, his tone more befitting a boy of three than a man in his thirties.

"You want to please *me?*" Sissy retorted, tossing her flowing mane of blond hair in mock anger. "You can please me by sticking those grab-happy hands inside your cup of buttered popcorn." After taking a sideward glance up into Foster's pouting face, the girl couldn't help giggling aloud. "Don't be so upset," she murmured sweetly, closing her lips against his ear and brushing a lobe with her tongue. "Maybe in two weeks, when I'm eighteen, I'll give you my virginity."

Foster inclined his head slightly and brought his lips against the girl's own moist lips. He caught the scent of some imported perfume she'd blown a month's allowance on as he took her Pepsi-sweetened tongue into his mouth. They kissed for a full moment, and this time Sissy didn't object when he slid his hand gently up her top.

Foster wondered a bit about her change of mind but didn't question it as he swept the side of his palm enticingly over her smooth belly. Seconds later, he had just poked one finger experimentally up her bra cup, when the houselights came on, signifying the movie's end. Sissy jumped reflexively in the sudden glare, startling Foster, whose other hand still clutched a nearly full barrel of buttered popcorn. A geyser of greasy popcorn cascaded into the air, covering two elderly ladies in the row in front of Foster.

"Oops, sorry!" Foster exclaimed. "I didn't mean to butter you ladies up."

The women, unfortunately, were not amused by his attempt at humor; they turned to give him and Sissy a large portion of their tiny minds. Foster hustled Sissy toward the aisle without looking back. "Do you believe the *words* coming out of two such sweet-looking old mouths?" he wondered aloud in shocked disbelief.

Once the couple reached the safety of the lobby, Foster helped his date on with her sweater. His hands lingered a long moment over her bare shoulders.

"Sissy?"

"I've been known to answer to that name."

"I got a question about your Uncle Tiny," Foster continued, ignoring her sarcasm. "What would he say if he knew I was going out with you, especially with your being jailbait and all?"

The journalist released an involuntary shudder as he pictured the menacing-looking bounty hunter advancing toward him with malice in his heart. Foster had seen Tiny in action many times, and he knew that it was suicide to tangle with him. The bounty hunter had made it all too clear that he'd rather sandpaper his own bleeding hemorrhoids than spend thirty consecutive seconds in Foster Foster's company. The two had grown up together in St. Jo, Missouri, but neither could think of another thing in common except for race and a mutual weakness for red-hot women.

Sissy took Foster aback with her response. "Oh, Uncle Tiny already knows we're dating. I've called him collect once a month ever since I can remember. He always knows *everything* about me."

"He does?" cried the exasperated writer. "What did he say when you told him?"

"He told me to start calling him once a *week* instead, to report on you. That is, once a week as long as you were good. But if you got out of line, Tiny said I should phone and he'd take the next plane to Missouri to give you a mountain skinning. I'm not sure what that exactly means, though. Do you know?"

"Uh, no," the writer lied weakly. He'd interviewed enough trappers for feature stories to know what mountain skinning was. It was when a man stuck his fist so far down your throat that he wrung you inside out by the toes. "Did Tiny say anything else?"

"Yeah," Sissy answered blithely. "He said your mother was a whore and your daddy was a pimp. That you was so unpopular as a kid that your mother used to tie a pork chop to your neck so's the family dog would play with you."

Foster kept one hand curled above Sissy's rib cage and brought the other up to his forehead. He tried kneading away a sudden headache as he escorted Sissy out of the theater onto Kansas City's main drag.

Sissy continued jabbering away. "But finally, after he called you about 894 bad names, Uncle Tiny admitted that you were good folks deep inside and that I could go out with you, on one condition."

"Which is?"

"That you keep your fucking paws to yourself," Sissy growled in her best gravel-voiced imitation of her uncle. She knocked away Foster's fingers, which somehow had levitated toward her breasts.

Foster was about to respond as he reached the darkened lot where he'd left his red Ford truck, but a sudden sense of uneasiness gripped him. A journalist who lived for dangerous and offbeat assignments, Foster had a way of sensing trouble just before it occurred. He peered uneasily into the darkness as he slipped the key into the passenger door without looking at it.

"Hurry up, Foster!" Sissy said impatiently. "What on earth are you waiting for?"

"I don't remember locking these doors up," Foster told her. "Or maybe it's just my imagination."

But when the door sprang open toward him, so did Foster's imagination, in the form of two men who had been lurking crouched down in the cab of the journalist's truck.

The first attacker, a black behemoth, held two fists intertwined together as he cracked Foster on his bearded chin, sending him crashing heavily against an adjacent car. The second attacker, a shabby-looking piece of white trash, grabbed on to Sissy, making sure to get two handfuls of breast, while the girl froze in shock. "Scream and you die, bitch!" the man hissed, slapping a filthy hand over her mouth.

Lying in a daze on the ground, Foster was aware of more fear than he'd ever felt before. A few inches from his face, restrained by a chain-link leash clutched by the third attacker who had been hiding in a nearby station wagon, a massive jaguar cat bared its yellow fangs ferociously. Sour breath covered Foster like San Francisco fog, and the click of the beast's teeth warned the writer that his face could easily be reduced to red pulp.

"Move, my friend, and your life is all hers," purred the jaguar's handler, speaking in a distinct musical cadence.

Foster kept still. A voice within him said to look for details about the three attackers, which he did, though his eyes kept returning involuntarily to the spear-sharp fangs a mere eighteen inches away.

Little details struck the writer, however: the beard and porkpie hat of the jaguar's handler, the bulk of the black man holding onto Sissy, the grimy clothing of the other white man, who was forcing a gag into her mouth.

The handler was the only one who had spoken, and it was clear that he was in charge. "Get the girl into the back seat of the station wagon," he barked, "and open up the cage for our friend, the jaguar."

"What about him?" asked the slimy-looking white man. "Should I kill him?"

"No, not necessary. Give him a little rest if you like."

Forcing himself to turn away from the cat's gleaming eyes, Foster rotated his head ninety degrees to meet his attacker and caught the crushing force of a revolver against his skull. A pained explosion of brilliant lights flashed in his brain, only to disappear instantly in a wash of absolute blackness that obliterated all pain.

*   *   *

Daylight struck before Foster regained consciousness. His head felt as though a buffalo had used it for a footrest. There was another pain in his gut, and he gradually became aware that his attackers had tossed him atop the floor shift of his truck. As he maneuvered onto the seat, his head banged into the steering wheel, sending flashing lights of pain directly to his brain.

It took Foster another ten minutes to get himself out the door of the cab. But when his legs hit the pavement, they proved too rubbery to support his 190 pounds. The writer swayed like a skyscraper in a wind storm and then crumpled forward onto his chin, skinning it.

As he lay there dazed, a strong pair of arms came out of nowhere to lift him to his feet. For the second time, Foster felt himself being thrown around. This time his sore head smashed into the front fender of the Ford.

As Foster sat dazed and in semishock, he forced some strength to emerge. When he felt a hand on his shoulder, about to toss him once again, Foster whirled and threw a hard right, which knocked his attacker's dick in the dirt.

But even as he swung, Foster saw that his tormentor was a young Kansas City patrolman. Holding his bleeding nose, the cop drew his service revolver and trained it square on the writer's pen pocket.

"Try it again, you fucking drunk," the young patrolman said with a sneer. "If you so much as hiccough, I'll air-condition you with this. Now take out your wallet—slow!—and show some ID."

Foster, his head aching, had lost all patience. He reached slowly into his back pocket and pulled out his billfold. He snapped open the photo section and handed it to the cop. The rookie's eyes bulged out at the stack of press cards: *The New York Times, Rolling Stone, Playboy, People* magazine, *Oui,* the *Atlantic*

Monthly. Foster served as contributing editor for each of these publications.

"Satisfied?" Foster barked at the kid. "Now get me your superiors and a doctor, in that order. There's been a kidnapping. If you hurry, maybe I won't write something that'll lose you that nice, shiny new badge."

Chapter Three

Hours passed before Tiny and Hammer could resume their twelve-hour drive to Denver. The highway patrol officer had called in the make and license of the pimp's truck and camper, but that had turned out to be a dead end. The vehicle had been stolen from a Grand Canyon parking area two weeks before. It was registered to a Methodist minister.

After giving every detail they could think of, Tiny and Hammer bid good-bye to the Highway Patrol investigators. The girl's family had been found after a phone call to local authorities in Fayetteville, and an older brother was on his way to make arrangements for shipping the body home.

Once behind the wheel of his newest motor home, baptized the "Wolfmobile," Tiny, for once, was as silent as Hammer. Not even an affectionate swipe of the tongue from Sidney the wolf could improve the bounty hunter's spirits. The motor home was well into central Utah before he could bring himself to voice his thoughts.

"You know, Hammer, in our business you got to deal with lowlifes of every stripe, but to my way of thinking, there ain't no skunk lower than a man who messes with kids."

Hammer nodded sympathetically.

"Can you imagine what kind of perverted twisted

mind takes a fourteen-year-old and has her sucking cock when she's supposed to be hugging dolls? I tell you, there'll come a day of reckoning, I can feel it. And if that motherfucking pimp Al or any of his cock-breath associates gets anywhere near me, I'll break off every one of their legs and arms and club 'em to death with the wet ends."

Darkness had long since settled when the Wolf-mobile pulled into a rest area outside Grand Junction, Colorado. "Go get yourself some exercise," Tiny urged Sidney as he let him outside, "but don't you go chomp-ing on some old lady's chihuahua."

Hammer hauled out a Coleman stove and set it out-side to cook some steaks. For November, the weather was remarkably warm. Both men had thrown on wool Pendleton shirts but kept their vests on instead of jackets. A half hour later, Tiny regained some of his good humor while munching on a side of sirloin.

"I got an idea, Hammer." Tiny chuckled. "After we get this here job done, why don't we head east to Mis-souri and see my niece Sissy? She's been going out with that rumdum writer Foster Foster, which I don't espe-cially object to other than we got enough dummies on my side of the family already. I'll bet Foster would just shit a baked brick if he saw us coming. Sissy tells me he rented a cabin south of St. Jo just to be near her."

Hammer and Tiny simultaneously stuck their buck knives into their second steaks on the grill, and each tossed the leavings from the first steak over to Sidney. "Did I ever tell you about how I brung Sissy up back in St. Jo?"

The quiet man nodded, indicating that Tiny had in-deed told that story.

"Well," Tiny insisted, "just shut the fuck up and lis-ten. I'm gonna tell you it again."

The bounty hunter leaned forward and poured him-self a cup of steaming black coffee. "After my parents kicked off in a car wreck when I was two, I lived in an orphanage for three years without anybody wanting to claim me. I mean, it started to get me down after a while. Every time some new couple would come in hoping to fetch away a kid, they'd line the whole kit and caboodle of us up for inspection like we was puppies in a dog pound. Well, naturally all the sweet-lookin' girls and ass lickin' boys got snatched up quick. Ain't nobody wanted a homely kid who looked like he could eat you straight into bankruptcy.

"Anyhows, after about eighty straight times of getting passed over, I began to wise up to the fact that I'd reach eighteen and still be an orphan unless I adopted some devious measures. So, what I did was strike a bargain with all the orphans on the playground. I told them that it's only fair *I* get chosen the next time. I was real tactful, of course. I explained how long it took for broken noses and black eyes to heal up, and all the boys and girls got cooperative in a hurry.

"The next Sunday, the dorm director puts the word out that a couple would be in the orphanage in an hour to check out us kids. Well, I tell you, them fellow orphans of mine was just as good as gold. Some of the kids dressed up in their dirtiest, most raggedy clothes. A few of 'em took headers into mud puddles and such. And then there was a couple of kids who clued me in as to how they'd throw a hell of a tantrum once they lined us up in a chorus line."

Tiny slurped down the last dregs of his coffee and lit a fresh cancer stick. "Well, in comes this couple who were somewhere in their midthirties. They'd already adopted one kid—my beloved singing brother, Jerry Jeffers—and thought one more orphan was just what they needed. Anyway, no sooner did they walk into the room than the shit smacked right into the fan. You've never seen such a circus in your life. All the orphanage directors was fit to be tied.

"I mean, here I was, dressed in a white shirt and tie, while all around me was the orneriest, sloppiest,

meanest bunch of little bastards you ever saw. I mean,
they was scrappin' and pullin' each other's hair and
lookin' about as dirty as slop hogs in a sty. And suddenly, right in the middle of the commotion, I stepped
forward and clapped my hands—just once—and everybody climbed back in line, gooder than any angel.

"Out of the corner of my eye, I could see that the
couple was goin' for it. And sure enough, they huddled
with one of the directors and picked me out right on
the spot. Well, that director, she was pissed, but there
weren't much she could do other than whip my ass
when she marched me back to fetch my gear. She
didn't know how, but she knew somehow I'd been the
one responsible for all the commotion, and it itched her
asshole to no end.

"Of course, the final joke was on me. Mr. and Mrs.
Thaddeus Ryder, the couple who adopted me, turned
out not to even have a pot to piss in. They was so
poor, they had to wait for Goodwill to have a sale
before they could buy me a pair of britches. I mean,
my clothes always had more patches than a cabbage
farm.

"But gettin' along to Sissy," Tiny continued, absently
stroking Sidney, who'd come over to cuddle beside him.
"Mrs. Ryder—I never have called her 'mom'—had a
younger sister named Tillie, who had a baby out of
wedlock when I was about sixteen. The kid's name
was Cecilia, which I couldn't even pronounce, let alone
spell, and so I gave her the nickname of Sissy, which
stuck with her. Since she didn't have no father or older
brother, I kind of took that role while she was growin'
up. In fact, after her mother died of hard livin' when
Sissy was six, the Ryders took her in to be raised,
which of course was long after I'd left home."

The bounty hunter lumbered to his feet to give Hammer a hand with the cleanup. "The long and short of
it is that I'd cut my left arm off right below this tattoo
for Sissy. Anything she wants to make her happy, she

can have, even if it means dating that four-eyed, son of a pup Foster Foster."

Hammer laughed and pulled out his tin of Copenhagen to select a generous pinch. Tiny stretched out a hand to join him.

"All this talking about home is making me homesick for Missouri," Tiny grumbled, getting up to help Hammer toss away the garbage they had created. "What do you say we get a good night's sleep right here, then polish off Jock Crews and get the hell over to the 'show-me' state for a visit?"

Chapter Four

Once again country singer Jerry Jeffers had been fired, but he wasn't overly upset. For one thing, his three-month gig backing up a paunchy, popular balladeer had included a recording session that had filled his pockets with enough change to last a year. For another, the pleasant pain in his knuckles caused Jerry to chuckle every time he thought about that selfsame balladeer going airborne over the top of a keyboard.

"Teach *him* to yell at me for taking out his wife," Jerry grumbled to the sweet young thing he was escorting out of Shirley's Bar, an expansive, single-room cabin set on a dirt road off Highway DD south of Kansas City.

Although the place needed renovating before it could qualify as a dive, Shirley's was a home away from home for Jerry whenever he got to K.C. Even on a bad night, Shirley's was the Hernando's Hideaway of ma-and-pa bars. For less than a five spot you could score a strip steak or pork tenderloin. On special occasions (such as when Jerry came to town), Shirley herself would whip out a batch of fried bull's nuts, which the faint of heart referred to as Rocky Mountain oysters. Somehow, despite the fact that you could fit the population within a three-mile radius of Shirley's into Burt Reynolds's shower stall, the place was always teeming with good-looking, available women. Tonight had turned out to be no exception. Jerry Jeffers threw open the back of his hitched trailer and pushed inside with a porcelain-skinned redhead who had a chest sweet as fudge.

"I hope you don't think I'm too easy," giggled the redhead, who went by the handle of Kitty.

"Oh, no!" Jerry replied, batting his eyelashes. "Not as long as you promise to still respect *me* in the morning."

Kitty laughed again, a throaty sound mellowed by just the right amount of alcohol to make her receptive to anything, but not enough to make her sick at the worst possible time. The sultry woman was perhaps twenty-five years old with crinkle lines formed only by laughter. Her sea-dark blue eyes were fast becoming used to the light, or rather the lack of light, in Jerry's camper. She saw that the trailer was filled with sheet-covered mattresses and that the walls were lined with mirrors.

"Pretty much of a setup, huh, John?"

"Jerry," corrected the singer.

"Jerry it is," Kitty replied agreeably. "My sexiest spot is the back of my neck. Would you mind kissing it for me?"

"Sure," Jerry said. "My sexiest spot is the tip of my cock. After I do you, do you think you might . . ."

"Consider it done," Kitty said, in a huskier tone. Her hands dropped down to her white blouse. Deftly, she popped open three buttons to reveal the plumpest of breasts trapped beneath a scoop bra. "I'll race you to see who undresses the fastest," she cried.

Jerry won handily and stood over her, his erection pointed toward her lips.

"You cheated!" Kitty told him, pouting. "You're not wearing any underwear." The redhead slipped her hands to her sides and pulled off her banana-yellow panties, the final garment holding Jerry back from joyous penetration.

"Remember what you said," Kitty murmured. "First you do me, and then"—she paused and inched forward to ease her cool mouth over the head of Jerry's cock, tickling its opening with a snakelike flicking motion of her tongue—"and then you get more of this."

Giggling again, Kitty rolled her naked body over and arched her backside ever so tantalizingly. Jerry eased himself in between the backs of her knees and lowered himself atop her. For twenty minutes he teased and played. His tongue caressed her magnificent back from the nape of her neck to her bottom cheeks, while his hands wandered below from boobs to oozing snatch. When he fit first one, then two, then three, and then four fingers inside her, she moaned and turned wet lips up to him to be kissed.

Jerry's engorged penis tingled each time it touched bare skin. At last he dropped his shaft between her plump buns, while his fingers diligently maneuvered in and out of her. As he whaled away, he heard dimly the sound of knocking in some other realm, in some other dimension, light years still to travel. With Kitty beneath him, thrusting like the bucking-horse machine at Gilley's, Jerry began to forget about everything, even his earlier request for oral sex. Fuck it, he thought as he pounded away between her cheeks. I'll just shoot a bull's-eye right here.

But Kitty had other ideas. "Now you," she cried huskily, "and then me again." She slipped her lithe body out from under Jerry; like a hawk after game, she dove straight for his cock. Her lips opened, and she guided him into her mouth, immediately unfolding an incredibly long tongue that seemed to wrap itself nearly around his engorged organ. Every sense within Jerry urged him to come then and there, to bathe her tonsils with a stream of white that would ease the pulsating ache in his nuts. Instead, he opted for maximum pleasure, willing the torrent back a minute longer. Only dimly was he aware of a more insistent knocking somewhere close by. Suddenly, like a housewife removing a clothespin from between her lips, Kitty popped Jerry's cock from her mouth and looked up quizzically.

"Someone's at the door, John," she said anxiously.

"I don't care," he gasped, "and my name is Jerry."

"Sorry."

"I don't care," he gasped again, more urgently this time. "Finish me."

"No. It's probably important," Kitty insisted, tossing on her shirt. "Come on, or else I'll get it," she added, packing her legs into her tight slacks.

Totally naked, frustrated, and already aware that his balls were turning blue, Jerry maneuvered himself to the trailer door and kicked it open. He looked outside with no effort to hide the erection curving toward his belly button. When he saw who the visitor was, he exploded.

"Foster Foster!" he spat disgustedly. "I might have known it was you. Like bad pennies and poor relations, you always show up at the damnedest times."

"Sorry, Jerry. It's urgent. Fuck her quick and meet me inside Shirley's."

Jerry noted the Marlin 30-30 in Foster's hands and the bruises across the writer's cheekbones. "Something big is in the wind, I take it."

Foster nodded. "It involves Tiny, you, me, and Sissy."

"All right. I'll be out in thirty seconds. Order us fresh beers inside Shirley's."

Foster slammed shut the trailer door. Jerry turned and looked expectantly at Kitty, who was just finishing a quick cosmetic touch-up of her face. "Come on," Jerry said urgently, his granite-hard erection pointed her way. "Help me lose this load."

"No way," Kitty told him. "You want to leave, you leave now. Hey! What are you doing?"

"If a man wants to get anyone done," Jerry grunted, furiously stroking his cock until a tremendous gusher of semen slammed across the room, "sometimes he's got to do it himself."

Once back in Shirley's, it took Jerry but three sips of Budweiser before Foster had convinced him that Sissy's life might not be worth a gum wrapper unless something was done immediately.

"Have you got hold of Tiny yet?" the singer asked.

"No. I've tried several times to reach him on the phone in his motor home, but I haven't been able to connect. I've left a half dozen messages with Tiny's boss, Joey Hudson, over at the bail-bond office in Hollywood."

"Joey say anything?"

"Yeah. Tiny's working to bring back a skip who supposedly offed his own daughter when he was free on bond."

"How come?"

"Not sure, exactly," Foster replied. "All I know is that witnesses saw him running from her seedy motel room, and when they went inside, they found the girl with her throat slashed right through the jugular."

"Jesus." Jerry whistled. "Hey, what kind of motor home is Tiny gallivanting around in these days?" he asked, changing the subject.

Tiny's friends found it nearly impossible to keep track of all his travel homes. The bounty hunter went through three or four a year. If they weren't being blown up by some desperado or another, they were being shot up, driven over cliffs, or simply worn out by the punishment incurred through the tracking of bail skips from one coast to another.

Foster signaled for two more beers, indicating to the barmaid that the bill should go on Jerry's tab. "Last I heard, he's driving a big Explorer," Foster responded at last. "He calls this one the 'Wolfmobile.' "

"The Wolfmobile? He sure comes up with some jive-ass names. Why the 'Wolfmobile?' "

"Boy, you *have* been on the road working for a spell, haven't you, Jer?"

"Yeah, why?" the singer asked, his curiosity piqued.

"Guess you haven't heard that Tiny and Hammer came into possession of a full-grown gray timber wolf that's been accompanying them on cases. Tiny says that the beast is like taking two extra guns along."

"How'd they get hold of a wolf, anyway?"

"They busted some Eskimo from Barrow, Alaska, who came down to southern California to hide out with his girlfriend. They were living in a cabin up in the San Jacinto Mountains someplace."

"What was he wanted for?"

"I don't know exactly. Maybe possession of stolen blubber. Anyway, this wolf was chained up in back, and when Tiny carted off the guy and his woman, the Eskimo begged him to take the beast so the authorities wouldn't destroy it."

"Is it gentle?"

"Gentle as a lamb with Tiny and Hammer. A killer with anyone else who comes near it."

"What's its name?"

"Sidney."

"S-S-Sidney?" Jerry stammered. "What the fuck kind of name is that for a wolf?"

"Don't blame me, blame the Eskimo." Foster chortled. "It was his bright idea to call the wolf that."

"Hey, speaking of calling, why don't you hop on the horn and try to give Tiny a ring at the motor home?"

"Sounds like a winner," Foster agreed. He unwound his legs from the barstool and ambled across the room to the phone. But as he thumbed open his leather phone book to Tiny's page, the front door to Shirley's burst open. Two burly young men in their twenties strode inside, one of them clutching a familiar-looking redhead. An ugly-looking bruise the size of a pancake was already turning to purple on the girl's face.

"Point him out," growled the first beeftrust, spinning the woman ahead of him. "Show me the son of a bitch who *forced* you into his camper."

Jerry put down his Budweiser and stood up. "Leave the girl alone," he said quietly.

The second bruiser, a handsome man were it not for his extra chin and the inner tube around his middle, grinned and turned to his partner. "I think we found us our man."

The two men stood facing Jerry, while Kitty ran sobbing into the night. "My woman and I had a fight this afternoon while we was having a drink over in Grandview at the Ramada Inn. She took my pickup and left me stranded. Clete here picked me up, and we've been searching every bar on both sides of the Missouri-Kansas border for her ever since."

"You own the rig with the trailer on the back?" asked the bruiser called Clete.

Jerry nodded, sizing up his two foes and looking for an opening. In the meantime, every patron who'd been sitting on the barstools in front of the long wooden bar had gotten up and walked away—everyone, that is, but the resident drunk, a fortyish windbag named Crazy Al, who was passed out three stools away from·Jerry.

"Guess that settles things, then," said the cuckold. "We pulled up just as she was crawling out your rig. Oh, and incidentally, it'll be a while before you fuck anyone back there again. Me and Clete pissed all over your sheets and busted up those kinky mirrors of yourn."

That was too much for Jerry. The singer exploded from the stool like a halfback knifing off tackle and buried his head in Clete's ample gut. The big man fell back with Jerry atop him, flailing away at his soft flesh. The second partner roared and picked up a meaty fist to drive into Jerry's exposed back, but the blow never connected. Foster, who had inched quietly over from the wall phone, now raced toward the man on the dead run, leaving his feet at the last instant to plant both boots in the man's groin.

Foster was the first one up, and he used his boots again and again to advantage, hammering away at his opponent's manhood with deadly effectiveness and finishing his bent body off with a knee to the throat. The writer whirled to help Jerry, but there was no need. The singer stood daubing a small cut on his lip with a blue bandana. At his feet, Clete lay moaning in a semiconscious stupor.

"Thought you'd never clean his coop, Foster," Jerry said with a grin.

The writer winked back. "I'll finish making that call to Tiny if you think you can stay out of trouble for two consecutive minutes. My rifle's checked behind the bar. That ought to keep these two baboons from arranging a rematch with you."

Chapter Five

Roughly six hundred miles west of Kansas City, in the mile-high city of Denver, Tiny Ryder's mobile phone rang again in the Wolfmobile, which, except for Sidney, was empty.

Tiny's traveling home was parked on Blake Street while he and Hammer were questioning anyone they could find who lived in the rundown hotel where Cheryl Crews had been slain by her own father. The bounty hunter was covering the same ground that local authorities had covered the night of the murder, yet he was able to find out where Jock Crews was hiding out in but one hour of questioning.

"Thanks, doll," Tiny growled to an almost-pretty streetwalker clad in snakeskin cowboy boots and a slit-to-the-thigh red dress. "Maybe next time I'll get to spend my money in a way I'd enjoy more."

"You do that, honey," the streetwalker chortled. "I'll give you my five-finger discount."

The bounty hunter laughed appreciatively and ambled off with Hammer back to the Wolfmobile. "Not a bad evening's work," Tiny said. "Fifty bucks in exchange for Crews's whereabouts."

Hammer, in spite of himself, flashed Tiny a dubious glance.

"I read you, Hammer," Tiny growled. "You're wonderin' what business I have bargaining with a whore. You think maybe she's sold me a bill of goods."

The quiet man nodded.

"Nah," Tiny insisted. "That's why I only offered her the street price for a trick to cough up the information. Fifty bucks—no more, no less. You offer a whore a night's wages, say 400 or 500 bucks, she's gonna take a chance on losing her dental work to lie. Nope, I'll bet you this silver conch on my hat against that fancy buck knife in your belt that our man is staying at the Northern Hotel in Fort Collins."

Hammer looked longingly at Tiny's hand-tooled conch and then at his own razor-sharp knife and sadly declined the bet. The bounty hunter never gambled: not with his life, not with his money, not with his time. He bet the sure things and bet them all the way. Hammer was no fool; he refused the bet.

Tiny and Hammer departed, stopping for lunch at the Regency Hotel. Thus fortified, they cruised along at fifty-five toward the college town of Fort Collins, arriving sometime after 3 P.M. at their destination. The bounty hunter and his partner parked the motor home alongside a stretch of land adjacent to the Colorado Southern Railway tracks and began their walk to the Northern Hotel. When they'd gotten fifty yards, the mobile phone began to ring. Both men hustled back, but the line was dead when they picked it up.

"Hell with it," Tiny mumbled. "If it's urgent, they'll ring again."

The Northern Hotel turned out to be one of those rare jewels that travelers who insisted that "the best surprise is no surprise" never find. Both men fell in love with the Art Deco stained-glass ceiling high above them as well as the wonderfully crafted antique furniture that filled the room. An adjacent dining room, also heightened in effect by a stained-glass ceiling, had been featured in a recent Hollywood flick called *One on One*.

"May I help you gentlemen?"

Tiny and Hammer, heads gaping upward at the mul-tihued ceiling like two hicks seeing the Empire State Building for the first time, turned toward the speaker with slight embarrassment. The voice was that of the Northern's owner, who turned out to be a practical businessman. Tiny quickly outlined Jock Crews's case history and showed the manager a photo that Joey Hudson had provided.

"Yeah, he's here, all right," the manager, a young fellow with a slight New England accent, confirmed. "Rented a suite to him myself the other day. Quiet dude. He paid in cash for two full weeks."

With a little negotiation, Tiny arranged to rent a room opposite Crews's apartment. He also obtained a key to Crews's suite, but only after leaving a substan-tial deposit in the manager's safe. "If there's any dam-age at all, you forfeit the whole bundle. If it's over that amount, I'll expect you to cover the tab."

Tiny agreed and asked the manager for one favor: that he go up first to ascertain whether Crews was in his room. "Done," said the manager and came back five minutes later to report the apartment empty.

"All right, Hammer," Tiny told his partner, "I'll wait here to make sure Crews doesn't arrive unexpected-like. You hustle back to the motor home and fetch Sidney, our guns, and two walkie-talkies."

The quiet man nodded and strode away over the car-peted floor, catching a glimpse in a large side mirror of his own massive bulk squeezed into an extra-large black shirt. In orange letters, under the Harley insignia, read Hammer's challenge to Japan. "Better a sister in a whorehouse," screamed the shirt, "than a brother aboard a Honda."

As he burst through the double doors, Hammer nearly decapitated a wizened old man who had fool-ishly paused in front of them to light a cigar. "Watch yourself," growled the old man from somewhere underneath the dirt-encrusted baseball cap he wore.

When Hammer returned with Sidney and an armload of weapons a few minutes later, Tiny and the manager were waiting for him near a stairway that was off limits to guests except in case of emergencies. Tiny took possession of Room 310 directly opposite Crews's 311 suite, which Hammer cautiously entered. "Sidney can keep me company," the bounty hunter said to Hammer.

After the manager left, Tiny set up a stakeout from his window, which covered all of North College Avenue for a block on either side. From his vantage point, directly opposite the Cow Paddy Restaurant, Tiny had an unimpeded view of anyone approaching the Northern.

The bed alongside the window upon which he settled was never made for Tiny's length and bulk, particularly when Sidney's 120 pounds of gently snoring wolf were squeezed alongside the bounty hunter.

Hours passed. The only activity came from Sidney, who was twitching mightily in a dream. "Go get 'em," Tiny whispered to the beast. "What you huntin', Sid? A big old bull moose?"

Tiny tried imagining what it must be like up in the frigid Arctic country, where wolves like Sidney still were lords and masters of the tundra. "If Joey ever has a skip up there," Tiny vowed to the big canine, "me, you, and Hammer are goin'."

Tiny tilted back his trademark broad-brimmed black hat, which had been a Billy Joe model until the bounty hunter had finished molding it the way he liked. "Think I'll see how old Hammer's doing across the way," he muttered aloud to no one in particular.

"Tiny T. Tiny talking," he growled into a walkie-talkie that looked like a toy in his massive hand. "Come on in, Hammer, the reception's fine."

Across the way, in Suite 311—an apartment that

was the size of four normal-sized rooms and had housed eight cadets during WW II when the U.S. Army controlled the Northern—Hammer merely grinned when Tiny came on the line.

"Can't fool me," Tiny boomed. "I know you're out there."

The bounty hunter switched to receive and caught a faint chuckle on the other end. "Sure glad the owner decided to cooperate and let us use these rooms. Guess it was my charm that won him over," mumbled Tiny. "Course the hundred-dollar bill I slipped him didn't hurt, neither."

The bounty hunter's mind switched gears to a joke he'd just remembered. "Hey, Hammer! Do you know what's the trouble with oral sex?" he rasped. "The view stinks." The big man chortled to himself and switched the button, hoping to hear a little appreciative laughter on the receiver. All he got was silence.

A minute later, Tiny's voice again broke over the line. This time he spoke with urgency. "Crews is on his way to the room, Hammer. I see him coming out of Washington's Bar down the street."

Hammer reached out and pulled his blue L. L. Bean watchcap down low over his fringe of sparse blond hair. He readied his custom Stoeger-Ferlach *Doppelbuechs Drilling,* a three-barrel rifle-shotgun combination weapon that could pick off a peanut across a football field without cross-firing. The quiet man knelt in readiness in the bathroom in view of the front door, a portable refrigerator in front of him to steady his weapon and block any return fire.

Also in his lap was a sawed-off sledgehammer, perfectly balanced, with one side of the head sharpened like a tomahawk. In close, Hammer could and had demolished up to six foes with ease. And woe to anyone who tried fleeing the quiet man's wrath. He once had hurled the hammer at a purse snatcher in downtown

L.A. and brought down the speeding youth with a direct hit that traveled thirty yards through the air.

Tiny's voice drifted over the line once again. "Get ready, partner. Another man came out of Washington's and just handed Crews a toothpick. I take it he's the skip's brother. Joey warned us Crews had kin here. Let's consider both of them dangerous."

Suddenly, there was a sharp rapping at Tiny's door. He set down the walkie-talkie and moved quietly toward the entranceway. Sidney rocked back on his haunches, every muscle tensed to leap. His white fangs showed cruelly through his bared lips, and one eye looked to Tiny for the signal that indicated attack.

Moving his body to one side of the door as a precaution against someone shooting through it, the bounty hunter jerked open the knob. Standing there was the same crusty old codger Hammer had accidentally run into earlier. Tiny took him to be the type who lives by the week in hotels all his life, the type you read about in the paper who dies in a cheap bed while smoking during a prolonged drinking bout.

The old visitor did a double-take when he saw Sidney poised for attack. The wolf's hair bristled, and his yellow eyes were slits of pure hatred. The geezer's chances of dying on the spot from a coronary increased dramatically when he spied Tiny's massive bulk all set to squash him like a louse.

"Just wanted to welcome you to the hotel," the old man mumbled. "Thought maybe you'd buy me a drink or something. I didn't mean nothing by it."

Tiny pondered the dilemma. Should he pull the old man inside until Crews was captured? Should he just let him go? By now Crews was inside the hotel, maybe even on the stairway, only a minute from walking into the trap. The bounty hunter shook his head and then decided against risking the old man's safety.

"Pop, get lost and buy yourself a drink on me," Tiny

growled, forking over a double sawbuck. "Git, afore my mind changes!"

"Y-y-yes, sir," the old man squealed, clutching the greenback while Tiny shut the door on him. The bounty hunter hustled to get the walkie-talkie.

"Crews and his brother are on their way up," he barked into the receiver with a fierceness that caused Sidney to bristle anew. "If they so much as lift an armpit, blow 'em to heaven and let 'em drop down to hell!"

The bounty hunter ran a hand over his long, slicked-back dark hair. Never was he more alive than when in danger. Not a man to use drugs, Tiny's sometimes daily flirtations with death were his only addiction.

Seconds ticked by, then minutes. Something was wrong, *very* wrong. The bounty hunter glanced over at Sidney, who showed not the slightest sign that any enemy was about.

Three more minutes ticked slowly by, and then all hell broke loose. Footsteps sounded clearly along the carpeted floor outside Tiny's room. Someone halted outside the door, and there was the thwock of an object dropped from a short distance. Tiny's keen ears heard another object drop, followed by the rapid steps of a trespasser fleeing.

Tiny's first reaction was to fling open the door, but years of instinct warned him that such a move might be foolhardy. As a precaution, he yanked back Sidney, who was snarling furiously at the door, and dragged the wolf into the far corner of the room. Huddled alongside a mirrorless dresser, the big man yanked a mattress off the bed to throw in front of himself and his beast. No sooner did he do so than two near-simultaneous explosions erupted.

Instantly, the door a few yards away dissolved into shrapnel, and dangerous pieces of jagged wood flew everywhere with enough force to skewer a man. Glass splattered out over the street from a half dozen third-floor windows.

Into Tiny's smoke-filled room dove a stocky man with a few days' growth smeared across his jaw, wearing a denim cap. Although dazed slightly by the concussion, Tiny realized that the intruder was Crews's brother. The bounty hunter whipped up his .357 magnum, shot twice, and watched the man's nose disintegrate.

Tiny bolted upright, as light on his feet as a dancer, and hurtled over the fallen Crews brother just as another figure pitched into the doorway. The newcomer was the old codger Tiny had previously sent away, but this time the man wasn't asking for a handout. He had a long-barreled .44 in his liver-spotted hand, and it was spitting puffs of yellow smoke.

"What the hell?" Tiny ejaculated just as a bullet whipped past him and buried itself in the dresser alongside Sidney, who was groggily trying to pull his wolf wits together after the explosion. The old man fired again, and this time the shot ripped through Tiny's massive nettle of beard, narrowly missing his neck. The smell of gunpowder was strong in the air, and the room was a disaster area.

Tiny fired from point-blank range but missed. The pause allowed the old codger to fire again, and this time the bullet slammed into Tiny's primer chain belt, saving his life but hurtling him backward as if he'd been tackled in a football game. As he fell, the bounty hunter fired from the hip, and this time his snap aim was true. The old man's beady eyes opened wide, and he looked up as if trying to gaze at the bloody hole that had just opened in his forehead. Before his corpse hit the ground, first Sidney—slightly unsteadily—and then Tiny pushed past him to assist Hammer.

Sidney's powerful legs reached Room 311 in a single stride, just as Jock Crews was about to blow the unconscious Hammer to kingdom come. The door to 311 had been blown apart in the second explosion, and

Hammer had been belted between the eyes by the metal door lock, which had been sent flying like grapeshot.

But even as Crews's hand stroked the trigger, his aim was thrown off. A shot plowed into the floor an inch from Hammer's face as a gray streak hit Crews like a thunderbolt. Sidney's momentum carried him and the man forward. They sailed together through a gaping hole that had contained a large window before the explosion.

Sidney's fall was only about seven feet. He bounced off a metal gutter, emitting a yelp like a punished puppy, and then bounced onto the asphalt roof. Only slightly shaken by the fall, the wolf recalled the hated man and looked around menacingly to finish him off. But though Sidney whirled about in confusion, the man was nowhere to be seen.

Tiny, however, peering down from the blown-out wall in Room 311, saw what had occurred. A hole in the large sun roof about five yards from the wolf's paws told the bounty hunter that Jock Crews had fallen through to the lobby. The big man pocketed his smoking gun and turned to assist Hammer, who was now in a sitting position, gingerly touching at his injured face.

"You all right, brother?" Tiny asked solicitously. "That goose egg on your head looks ready to hatch."

Hammer shook his head to indicate that he was all right and wobbled over to pick up his cherished weapon. Shrugging off any further aid, the quiet man accompanied his partner down three flights of stairs to the lobby, pausing to regain Sidney's company by letting the wolf in through a second-story window. When the canine bounded happily inside, Hammer bent to pound the beast affectionately atop its heavily furred head, while Tiny drew out a gift of dried jerky from a compartment in his biker's wallet.

A few seconds later, the unlikely-looking trio reached the lobby to find that pandemonium reigned.

A half dozen well-dressed women who had come to the Northern's fancy restaurant to eat now stood off to one side or collapsed into leather chairs, shaken and tearful. A few yards away, several businessmen in ties and jackets were looking around in bewilderment.

On the hand-polished wooden floor, bent and broken like a long-forgotten toy, lay the body of Jock Crews. High above, cut as if with a cookie punch in the stained-glass Art Deco ceiling, was the shape of the armed robber's spread-eagled body. A grotesque red stain covered his clothing, seeping into the floor and growing into an ever larger puddle.

Overseeing the body, though obviously befuddled and angry, was the hotel's youngish manager, who strode purposefully toward Tiny and Hammer until a warning growl from Sidney caused him to jump back.

"Now don't get upset," Tiny told him in as soothing a voice as his harsh baritone could muster. "Here's a pile of hundreds," he said, ejecting them from his wallet, "and the business card of my boss, Joey Hudson. Find out the extent of the damage, and he'll cover it as a matter of course."

"All right," the manager said, placated by the sudden appearance of green in his hand. "You'll have some explaining to do with the police, too. I called them."

"Fine, fine!" said Tiny. "You just saved me the trouble of getting to the phone. But now I have a question," he added. "Just who the hell is that dangerous old man you got wandering around here? His dead ass is flopped over in my room."

"Don't know much about him except that he's been living here nearly six months. His name is Ben Crews, and I take it his son Jock over there was the man you were hunting."

Tiny brought a massive paw to his eyes and kneaded them as if trying to prevent them from dropping out of his skull. "Boy," he said sardonically, "I guess you'll rent a room to anybody."

The owner stared Tiny right back in the eye. "Sure," he replied, "I rented one to *you,* didn't I?"

A sudden piercing scream from one of the female onlookers caused Tiny to jerk around with his guns drawn for action. "He moved," the woman insisted, pointing to Jock Crews's body. "He's alive."

The bounty hunter hustled over and saw that the woman was right. Crews had somehow survived the fall. "Get a doctor!" Tiny commanded the onlookers, and a half dozen people jumped to comply. The big man cradled Crews's broken form in his arms.

"Don't try to talk," Tiny cautioned him.

"Water," the man moaned. The manager nodded to Tiny and scurried off to the nearby kitchen.

"Cheryl—my daughter," Crews gasped.

"Yeah," Tiny answered, his voice hardening. "She's dead. You killed her."

A storm of tears welled up in Crews's eyes, and a red stream of blood leading to but one conclusion flowed out both sides of his mouth, onto the bounty hunter's jeans.

"I . . . didn't . . . kill her," the dying man sobbed.

Tiny looked sternly into the fast-clouding eyes of the man who five minutes earlier had tried to blow him to hell. "I believe you. You got no cause to lie now. But if you didn't kill her, who did?"

Crews's blood-rimmed eyes bulged white, and he shivered violently in Tiny's grasp as if the devil himself were right there to drag him to damnation. Hammer, with Sidney in tow, looked sympathetically down at their former enemy as he fought to squeeze out his last sentence on this earth.

"The . . . Jaguar . . . killed her," Crews moaned, just as one final torrent of black blood burst forth from his heart.

Chapter Six

Sissy's first twenty-four hours of captivity were filled with unmitigated terror. Once thrown into the back of the vehicle with a strong-armed captor on either side of her, she had no doubt that she'd be used cruelly. A dirty handkerchief that stank of oil had been stuffed roughly into her pretty mouth, and her hands were bound firmly.

The car had not been five minutes on the road before Sissy's tank top was jerked savagely up to her armpits, leaving her breasts exposed. Rough hands tore at her light, near-translucent nipples, and she had to endure the coarse judgments of them by the others in the car. After a while, just one man played with her breasts, and she endured the hot scent of his breath as he sucked her neck from time to time.

A while passed, and then the other man took his turn, but he soon moved to Sissy's lower extremities, forcing her legs open by painfully grasping the loose flesh along her thighs. Soon he had her white tennis shorts unzipped and had pulled them to her knees. All that remained was a pair of flesh-colored panties, and they soon were cut away with one slash of the man's knife.

Where no man's hand had ever been, suddenly there were two.

"Hey, it's my turn," one man growled. "Ain't my fault if you stopped just with her titties."

A rough thumb traced the outline of Sissy's tight opening, disappeared for a second, and then came back loaded with moisture from his mouth. With slight effort, he worked his finger inside her experimentally and then pulled it out as if it had been bitten on the inside.

"Holy shit!" he exclaimed. "This one's a virgin."

Rough hands, on both sides this time, jerked down Sissy's red top and pulled up her shorts to their former position.

"We got to deliver this one straight to the boss," said the jaguar handler in his stern but melodic voice from the front seat. "If either of you two louses touches her again, I'll sic this big cat on you."

Chapter Seven

Stakeouts and flying bullets he could endure, but Tiny was bone-tired during a meeting with Larimer County law enforcement authorities to answer a thousand questions and fill out twenty pages of forms. As usual, he had to endure the ignorance of local yokels unfamiliar with the rights and procedures of bounty hunting. Since Tiny wore denim and leather and since his arms bore the work of many a tattoo artist, a few cops itched for a chance to toss the big man's hide into jail.

It got so that he could predict the questions. Lord knows, he had given the answers often enough.

"Yeah, I got every right to go after a man who's skipped bail on my boss," Tiny informed several gum-chewing sheriff's deputies. "I work under the protection of an 1873 Supreme Court decision called *Tainter* v. *Tainter*, which states that I, as an employee of a certified bondsman, become a prisoner's jailer when he's out on bail."

"Maybe you're right," drawled a lantern-jawed officer in his late forties, "but I'll have to lock you up until I get a law book and look up that decision."

"No need," Tiny insisted, barely hiding his impatience. He popped open his black leather briefcase, stained with the blood of feisty skips on all four corners, and hauled out a file folder filled with Xeroxed pages. "These here are from the Orange County Law

Library," he said. "This is a copy of the *Tainter* v. *Tainter* decision. You can keep it; I got an extree."

"Maybe so," the officer said, glancing down at the sheet disappointedly, "but we got local ordinances covering the carrying of weapons. There's no way you boys can get away with carrying all that heat."

"Sorry," Tiny said, handing the officers another Xeroxed sheet. "The exception to carrying a loaded firearm in a public place in Colorado is if I am carrying out official duties, which I am. Hammer here or anyone else assisting me on a case is also so empowered."

A short stocky officer interrupted the bounty hunter. "You got anything that says you can go around shooting anybody you goddamn well please?"

"Nope, not anybody I damn well please," Tiny amicably said, "just anyone who presents a clear and present danger to my life and well-being." The bounty hunter thumbed around a bit and then handed two more Xeroxed sheets over. "And I do happen to know my legal rights when it comes to questioning. So unless you boys here and now want to charge me with something, I'll be just happier than a rooster in a full henhouse to get the hell out of your town right now."

"All right, Mr. Ryder," the lantern-jawed officer said with a scowl. "We'd be even more thrilled to have you vacate our state. You and your friend are free to go." He smiled as a sudden thought came to him. "Providing, of course, you got a U.S. Department of Wildlife permit to cart around that wolf of yours."

The bounty hunter glanced down at Sidney and breathed silent thanks that his boss, Joey Hudson, had insisted that he pick up a permit for the wolf. Tiny reached into his briefcase for yet another folder and hauled out the appropriate document. "Good-bye, boys," Tiny rasped. "It was awful kind of you to invite me to stay overnight in your jail, but maybe next time you'll be a little better prepared."

*   *   *

Back at the motor home, Tiny fed and watered Sidney and then mixed a salad and three cold beef sandwiches apiece for himself and Hammer. "Start that engine up pronto, partner," Tiny rumbled, "and put us on the road to K.C. My guess is that those boys will come inspect this motor home for certain if we lolly-gag around here. And the way that one deputy sheriff was shooting bullets with his eyes, they'd like as not give us twenty years for having a busted tail light."

In two hours the Wolfmobile was winging east along Interstate 70, with Tiny behind the wheel. The bounty hunter had taken the first snooze until Denver and then had traded places with his partner.

On a sudden inspiration, Tiny reached for his brief-case and removed a small leather-bound book. Thumbing through the pages with one eye on the highway, he found the number he wanted and gave the information to the FCC operator.

The call went through in a few minutes.

"Howdy, darling," Tiny said. "Is this Mary, the girl of my dreams, the love of my heart, the woman with whom my soul is complete?"

Getting an affirmative response, Tiny kept pouring on the coal while Hammer listened with one eye and one ear opened in his bunk.

"Yeah, darling. I tell you, if you was any purtier, God wouldn't have sent you down to earth. Nope, he would have kept you all to himself."

The bounty hunter smiled in self-congratulation at his powers of oratory, but in a second his face became a disturbed mask.

"What do you mean, you're six months pregnant?" Tiny roared. Then, a sudden horrifying thought rattled through his skull, and he spoke again in a more subdued tone. "Um—it wasn't me the last time through K.C. that turned you into a mother, I hope?"

Tiny winced and waited for her answer. Hammer now had both eyes open.

"Oh, that's good, whew! Well then," he said, his voice hardening. "You tell me who the shiftless prick is who done you wrong, and we'll set him straight in a hurry."

The bounty hunter's jaw dropped when he got his answer. "Your *husband* is the father? Shit, I *guess* it's been a while since I poured through Missouri."

Tiny was about to put back the phone when another thought came to him. "Say, Mary, seeing how you's all taken, what are the chances of you fixing me up with that purty twenty-year-old sister of yours, the one with the big titties?"

The bounty hunter waited in anticipation but then gave a puzzled look at the phone. He turned when a small chuckle from the back warned him that Hammer had been eavesdropping. "She hung up," Tiny said in amazement. "I wonder if it was something I said?"

Still shaking his head in bafflement, Tiny replaced the phone, only to have it ring while still in his hand. "Tiny here," he rasped.

"Yes, sir," an official-sounding voice announced. "This is your FCC operator calling back. I really must warn you about your use of language on the line. It is my job to monitor these calls, and any other violation could cost you the privilege of maintaining a mobile phone."

The bounty hunter was annoyed and not a little perplexed. "Wait a minute," he said. "I was just talking to a lady. I don't recollect using *any* cuss words."

"I'm sorry, sir, you said three bad words."

"Three!"

"Yes, sir. One 'prick,' one 'shit,' and one 'big titties.' "

"Oh, excuse me," the bounty hunter giggled, not knowing whether to be embarrassed or burst out laughing. "I can assure you it won't happen again."

"Thank you, sir. I appreciate your cooperation."

"You bet, darlin'. You can kick my ass from here to

Missouri if I say another bad word." The bounty hunter put back the receiver, pleased with himself for being such a good citizen.

Again the phone rang, with no more than a two-second pause. "Grand Central Station," Tiny said cheerfully. "This is the head choo-choo."

"Hey, head choo-choo," drawled a familiar-sounding voice. "This is your friendly caboose, Jerry Jeffers."

"Why, howdy, Jerry!" Tiny exclaimed. "You always was the rear end of our friendship, wasn't you?"

"Why you slack-bellied, mother's son of a . . ."

"Whoa, whoa," Tiny screamed anxiously into the receiver. "The FCC operator is listening to this conversation. She said she'll bust me sure if there's any cuss words." Tiny altered his voice to sound a bit more sugary. "Uh, darling? Operator? Are you there?"

"Yes, I am."

"Ain't you goin' to bust me if I say any dirty words?"

"That's right."

"OK, operator," Tiny continued in his normal, below-sea-level voice. "You hear that, Jerry? Mind your p's and q's."

"You got it, Tiny," said the singer, but then his voice grew serious. "Listen, big man. There's a problem. Have you taken care of your business in Colorado?"

"Sure have. In fact, I got the nose of this bus turned toward Missouri right now. Why? What's up?"

"Well, I got Foster Foster here with me."

"No wonder you got problems. What's he up to now, that no-good, four-eyed, flea-bitten . . ."

"Hold on, Tiny," Jerry cried. "Don't forget about the FCC operator. Besides, Foster didn't do anything this time."

"He ain't done nothin' to our little Sissy, has he?"

"No, *he* didn't do anything. It's about Sissy, though.

If you're headin' this way, maybe I should wait until you get here."

"Don't do that to me, Jeffers. I'll worry every inch of the way out there, expecting the worst."

"Brace yourself, brother," Jerry said softly. "It *is* the worst."

"Hammer," Tiny called softly over his shoulder, "take over the wheel." The Wolfmobile pulled over to the side of the interstate, and the switch was made quickly. "Go ahead, Jerry."

"Sissy's been abducted by a gang of three men. Foster was with her when it happened. He tried to stop them, but they bushwhacked him. One of the men had a full-grown jaguar on a leash."

"A jaguar?" Tiny stammered.

"That's right. Foster says that if he would've twitched wrong, the cat would've ate him for lunch."

"Have the Ryders been contacted for ransom?"

"No dice. The local law out here figures she's been kidnapped by some sophisticated white slavers. I hate to say it, brother, but me and Foster tend to agree with 'em."

"When I get my hands on those . . . !" Tiny stopped himself suddenly. "I can't say what I'm really thinking, Jerry. The operator's listening."

Suddenly, the angry voice of the operator came onto the line. "Don't you worry about it. I heard every word your partner said. Go get those sons of bitches, Tiny!"

Chapter Eight

Darkness still reigned when the Wolfmobile hauled ass into the Trimble, Missouri, homestead of the Ryders, located between Kansas City and St. Joseph. The spread was an eleven-acre farm that Tiny had purchased for his foster parents with the first earnings his boss had given him.

"Yeah, it ain't exactly paradise, but it sure beats to hell that bottomland pigsty I growed up on," Tiny said to Hammer as they stepped outside into the forty-degree cold.

By the time the two big men hit the front porch, Jerry and Foster—both clad in shorts and thermal shirts—had hustled out to greet them.

"Come on in, brothers," said Jerry after neck-breaking bearhugs had been delivered to both men. "The folks are throwing on a pot of coffee."

"Howdy, Tiny. Hey, Hammer!" ejaculated Foster. "I ain't seen nobody as big as you guys since I did a story on a fat farm."

Tiny peered hard through the darkness as if he were having trouble placing the face and voice before him. "Well, god damn!" he chortled heartily. "It's Foster! I thought maybe the folks had hired themselves a skinny-assed cook or something."

At an oak table large enough around for King Arthur's knights, Tiny rejoined his family for the first time in many months. He took in the newest tucks and sags in the faces of Thaddeus and Madaline Ryder, his foster parents, and was newly aware of their mortality. Jerry looked the same as ever; he never aged. The boyish good looks that had earned him many tableside propositions were still intact, particularly his shit-eating grin, which popped up whether he was happy or low. The singer never could stay depressed for very long.

Foster, always aware of style trends, had changed. His once-long hair was trimmed short, and he had begun to grow a dark beard. "What's with them chin whiskers?" Tiny asked. "Didn't you look enough like a billy goat before?"

The writer grinned. "Nice to see you again, Tiny," he said. "I haven't been insulted in a long time."

"Oh, I'm sure you've been insulted," Tiny retorted. "You just wasn't smart enough to catch on is all. There's never been another man who so *invites* insults like you, Foster."

The talk, after the preliminary familiarities, quickly moved on to the subject of Sissy. Foster retold his tale, taking pains to remember every detail.

"What I'm most certain about are the voices of the three men. I'd know that singsong tone anywhere," the writer said. "They're from the south of Louisiana— Cajun and Creole country. I spent some time in that area doing a magazine article on a leper colony there."

"Wait a minute," croaked old Thaddeus Ryder. "I never could get those two straight. What's the difference between a Cajun and a Creole?"

"Well, this is simplifying it too much, maybe," Foster explained, pouring out his third cup of chicory-flavored coffee, "but it's sort of like the Creoles always thought they were God's gift to mankind. And maybe they were in a lot of ways. They were of French descent, and many disdained to ever learn the English language back in the days of the pirate Jean Lafitte. They were wealthy suckers—the plantation owners, the bankers, the politicians—and they didn't hold much regard for the Cajuns, who were descendants of a French group who escaped Canada because of religious persecution. They spoke a sort of pidgin French which the high-falooting Creoles sniffed at."

"So the Creoles are high-class and the Cajuns are low-class?" Thaddeus asked.

"It depends on how you look at it," Jerry Jeffers chipped in. "The Cajuns are earth-smart. They take tons of seafood out of the ocean in that season and then trap muskrats and other fur animals in winter. I've got nothing but respect for the way they've stayed their own men."

"Of course, the Cajuns have already joined the twentieth century in many ways," interjected Foster. "Some of them are quite famous for what they do. Ron Guidry of the Yankee baseball team and the singer Doug Kershaw are about the most famous Cajuns."

"To me it don't matter if they're Creole or Cajun," Tiny said, belching. "They're all coonasses, the salt of the earth. I like their cookin', their fun lovin', and their wimmens."

This last word was accompanied by a Groucho Marx uplifting of the eyes. But Tiny's grin quickly faded. "Hey, Foster," he said, changing the subject. "Didn't you say those men were laying for you in your truck?"

"Two of them were," Foster agreed, "a big black man with huge arms and a guy who smelled like he came out of a swamp. The third guy, the man who held back the jaguar, was hidden away someplace else in the parking lot."

"Did you check your truck for clues?"

"No, I went back to the parking lot with the cops investigating the case. No one thought to look in the truck."

"Well, put on your pants, Foster, and take us out

there," Tiny said impatiently. "Let's get on the stick. This case is now officially open."

Jerry and Foster scrambled away from the table to get their clothes while Tiny put his massive paw on the hand of his adopted mother. "Don't you worry, Mrs. R.," he said. "We'll find Sissy, and when we do, there's going to be dead bodies spread all over hell if anyone's so much as touched a blond hair on her head. I usually track men down for money, but this time I'm tracking them down for love. God help anyone who tries getting in our way."

The first hint of dawn was breaking through the inky blackness when Tiny and his three men sauntered out to Foster's truck. The writer turned on lights inside the vehicle and the attached camper in back.

"They were only up front, not in the back, is that right, Foster?" asked Tiny.

"Yeah, somehow they scrunched themselves down low so you couldn't see them from the door window outside."

Tiny pushed his bulk onto the floor and shone a flashlight under the seat.

"What you hoping to find?" Jerry asked.

"They had to do *something* while waiting for Sissy and Foster to come back. Obviously, someone had his eye on Sissy for a while before she was kidnapped. Otherwise, they wouldn't have known enough to hide out in Foster's truck."

The bounty hunter poked and probed under the seat. He pushed out several beer cans, crushed maps, and assorted garbage onto the mat. "Sure keep a tidy truck, don't you, Foster?" he grumbled. "Wait! Here's something. What kind of beer you drink?"

"Budweiser usually. Imported beer when I can find it."

"How 'bout Dixie beer?"

"Only had that once, when I was down in New Orleans. Tastes like panther piss as I recall."

Tiny sat up and tossed a Dixie can at the writer, who caught it on the fly. "Make that jaguar piss instead, Foster. We're headed to New Orleans. Hammer, warm up the Wolfmobile. We leave in ten minutes, boys."

Chapter Nine

With four drivers alternating shifts, the Wolfmobile made the run from Missouri to New Orleans in sixteen hours. With difficulty, Jerry managed to fit the motor home into a parking spot on North Peters near the Mississippi River ferry crossing, and then the men departed on foot to check out the French Quarter.

"Sorry, Sidney," said Tiny. "You go to sleep and guard the truck. I'll take you for a long run tomorrow."

"Ain't even midnight yet," Jerry said, glancing at his watch. "The night's young, so are we, and who knows what's in store."

"Whores," Tiny said.

"Oh, yeah?" Foster asked. "You horny, Tiny?"

"No, dummy," Tiny responded, smacking Foster on top of his ever-present Yankee batting helmet. "We ain't going to fuck them, we're going to question them. We got to find one that can lead us to Sissy."

The four walked around the Old Square, admiring the fine wrought iron-railed homes and the wealth of fine-assed women scurrying about in search of a party. The sound of good jazz poured out from every doorway, it seemed, and the scent of roux-laced cooking attacked every nostril.

"I can't stand it," Tiny said, leading his cohorts into a restaurant called La Boucherie on the corner of

Chartres and Conti. "I just got to get some gumbo into my stomach."

For an hour, the four men put away bowl after bowl of spicy food, savoring each succulent morsel. "They could lock me in a dungeon for twenty-four years," mumbled Jerry with a full mouth, "but as long as they fed me this stuff, I'd never complain."

"You said it," Tiny agreed, accepting his fourth heaping bowl from a bug-eyed waiter. "This reminds me of the way we used to chow down in St. Jo at this steak café owned by a guy named Lang."

"Yeah," the singer chuckled, explaining for Hammer's benefit. "You would've loved this place, Hammer. Every Friday, Old Man Lang offered this seventy-two-ounce steak special. If you could eat the whole meal—salad, taters, and meat—you didn't have to pay a dime. The whole thing was free."

"Me and Jerry went there every Friday for almost a half year when we was kids," Tiny continued. "And not once did we fail to finish a meal."

"We couldn't afford not to eat," Jerry chortled. "That steak dinner cost damn near a twenty-dollar bill if you couldn't finish it. And we used to walk into that place without a dime in our pockets."

"I remember that steak house, too," Foster said. "I tried it once but only ended up puking. There was no way to finish the damn thing, so I had to cough up twenty bucks, which I didn't have."

"Did you wash the dishes, Foster?" asked Tiny.

"Nah, I played the Galloping Gourmet and ran out the door," the journalist answered, chuckling.

"Old Man Lang would have been tickled to death if either me or Jerry couldn't come back to his place," Tiny said. "Remember how he finally started serving us seventy-six- and seventy-eight-ounce steaks after a while, hoping to slow us down? He couldn't believe it when we even put those away."

"I cheated once, though," Jerry admitted. "I had to

stick a hunk of steak in my boot when Lang wasn't looking."

"Finally, me and Jerry got bought off, though," said Tiny sadly. "The owner gave us $30 cash apiece not to eat there no more. We was broke and the sight of all that money won us over. We never ate there again."

The bounty hunter signaled for the check, mentally added a twenty-five percent tip, and peeled a thick slab of hundreds out of his chain wallet. "All right, boys. Let's hit the streets again."

As they left the restaurant, the four men were accosted immediately by two hookers in their forties who worked the Exchange Alley area. "No thanks, darlings," said Tiny, gently rebuffing them. "We're not buying tonight."

"What do you mean we're not buying?" Foster asked after the tarts had sashayed off. "How come you didn't ask them any questions?"

"We're looking for one specific pimp," Tiny explained. "We want the one who kidnapped Sissy and no one else. There's a couple dozen of what you call popcorn pimps on these streets with only one or two girls working for them. Our boy, obviously, is a big-time pimp since he's got strongarm men as well as girls on his payroll. He's also got to be a hell of a visible cocksucker if he's using a jaguar to help with his dirty work."

"Yeah." Jerry nodded. "Some high class young whore around here either works for him or knows of him. We just got to make the rounds, is all."

The four continued their prowling around the French Quarter until Foster suddenly stiffened when he saw a man and a heavily made-up woman talking angrily in front of a funky bar called the Dream Palace. "Tiny," he said urgently. "That's one of the guys who jumped me. I'd know that beard and porkpie hat of his anywhere."

Without another word Foster began racing down

Esplanade Avenue, with the other three men on his heels. Just at that moment, however, the target of Foster's fury looked up to see the writer bearing down on him and took to his heels, leaving the woman behind.

"Stay with him," Tiny ordered Foster and Hammer. "Jerry will get the motor home, and I'll stay here with the girl."

The bounty hunter looked over at Jerry, who was shaking his head from side to side. "This ain't no girl," Jerry said, eyeing the heavily rouged figure before him. "Look underneath her chin. She's got an Adam's apple."

It took Tiny a second to catch on. "Oh," he groaned in disgust, "you mean we got something in drag!"

"Hi, boys!" the queen lisped, winking at the stunned looks on the faces of Tiny and Jerry. "New in town?"

Chapter Ten

Foster, a former track man who still jogged daily, managed to keep up with Sissy's abductor as the chase turned down Bourbon Street. But as the writer jostled past some tourists lined up for entrance into Al Hirt's Club, he saw to his dismay that Hammer was no longer behind him.

The two men footraced south down Bourbon and then headed west toward the midcity district. Foster's legs and throat were starting to ache, but he didn't dare slow down. The writer wondered briefly whether his foe was armed, and he breathed silent thanks to Tiny for lending him the Browning 9-mm high-powered automatic now securely in place in a shoulder rig.

"Don't worry about taking on even a jaguar with this baby," Tiny had said. "This could even penetrate an engine block and crack it. The bullets are mail-order jobs I got special. They're Teflon-coated, armor-piercing babies, and they're expensive as hell, so don't waste ammo."

Foster's lungs began to burn in the damp midnight air as the chase continued through a residential neighborhood in central New Orleans. The writer gave silent thanks when he felt his second wind coming. Less than a block separated the two men when Foster heard squealing tires alongside him and saw Hammer leap out of a moving taxi to rejoin the pursuit.

The streets of New Orleans flew by the three huffing figures: Clark, Genois, Telemachus, Cortez. Scott Street came up, and Hammer began to lag behind his slimmer fellow runner. Tiny liked to kid Hammer that the quiet man had the speed and mobility of a double-wide trailer.

Suddenly, on Pierce Street, the pursued man bore right, losing his porkpie hat as he headed north. Finally, he legged it into the driveway of an ancient, red-brick home. Foster, a good fifty yards behind, drew his weapon and barreled up the driveway after the fugitive. The writer glanced backward for a look down Pierce Street and paused, wondering whether he should wait thirty seconds or so for Hammer to catch up.

"Fuck it," the writer said aloud. "I don't want him to get away."

His decision was very costly.

The writer threw open a heavy windowless door that the fleeing man had left unlocked and found himself in front of a narrow stairway leading from the entrance. When he looked up the dark stairs, he heard a melodic laugh from the man he had been pursuing and saw two giant fiery yellow orbs hurtling down at him.

The writer, his Browning 9 mm already pointed ahead, fired instinctively just as better than two hundred pounds of snarling fury slammed into him.

"The jaguar again!" Foster gulped. Those were his last words as an explosion of pain filled his brain, and his chest cavity ached as though a jackhammer had come down on it. Dimly he was aware of claws capable of disemboweling a bull raking into his down vest, aware of the beast's hot breath, potent enough to strip the enamel off a car.

In his entire life Foster had never before cried out in terror, but such was his horror that a piercing baritone shriek burst forth from him that chilled Hammer's blood as he huffed into the driveway.

Then Foster was still, deathly still.

Chapter Eleven

With eyes that had turned red-rimmed and lined with salt after days of weeping, Sissy huddled her fatigue-ridden body into the corner of a begrimed apartment, unfurnished except for a broken-down leather sofa, upon which reclined the giant black brute who had helped snatch her away from Foster.

The captor had stripped Sissy of all clothing and had chained her, with a collar strapped to her neck that smelled nauseatingly like cat. Sissy was acutely aware of the man's eyes upon her nipples, which showed clearly through her abundant but now filthy blond hair that she had draped over her chest in a vain effort to preserve some modesty.

Sissy had lost all awareness of time and had no idea of where she was being kept prisoner. All she had eaten had been a few crackers that the brute had bounced onto her lap and a gallon jug of silty warm water. Her stomach and kidneys ached. The last time she had gone to use the toilet, the giant had watched her with an openly contemptuous leer across his face. Naturally high-spirited, she felt so demeaned that the only sound that escaped her lips was a weak sob.

After two days in the room, the captive's need for sleep finally overcame her fear of the brute. But in the midst of a gruesome nightmare, she awoke to find that the giant had jerked her sideways and was lapping at her chest and pubes with his tongue. Too weakened even to scream, Sissy was only able to club weakly at the massive shoulders of the man as he buried his face into her triangular patch of pubic hair and shoved a thick tongue partially up her cleft. Sissy had once held secret fantasies about being raped, but always the rapist in her dreams had been one superstar actor or another. This, however, was a totally terrifying experience. The girl was powerless in the hands of a man fully capable of ending her life with the impact of one brawny forearm.

Sissy's eyes flashed open as the man's tongue darted inside her, and she looked up into the face of a second man. She recognized him immediately. It was the slovenly-dressed man who had helped this brute and the bearded man abduct her from Missouri.

"Help me, please!" Sissy whispered hoarsely.

Even the scruffy man apparently had a compunction or two left. "The boss ain't gonna like you messing with this girl, seeing how she's a virgin and everything," the man said in a whimpering tone that clearly revealed his fear of the other.

"He ain't never goin' to find out, though, Blinky," growled the brute, lifting up a wet chin from Sissy's body. "Especially since I'm going to fix it so's you don't dare turn squealer."

The giant rose and grabbed Blinky by the scraggly hair in back and shook him the way a coyote tosses a mouse. Then he dropped to one knee and shoved his companion purposefully toward Sissy.

"Hey! Don't do that, Jax," Blinky squealed as the brute ground the other's unshaven face roughly into Sissy's silky patch.

"I can't hear you too good, Blinky," Jax guffawed. "Not when you got your mouth stuffed with all that poontang."

Blinky struggled for another few seconds, until the animal lust in him took over, and then he duplicated Jax's oral attack of a few minutes before.

"Admit it," Jax guffawed in a voice that echoed in the unfurnished hovel. "That's got to be the best-eating pussy you've ever had." The giant smacked his thick lips obscenely. "I've been itching to do that ever since we drug her down here."

Too worn out to cry, Sissy patiently endured the foul-smelling Blinky's assault until the knowledge came that something warm and sticky was splashing into her face. "Oh, God, help me!" she moaned when she opened her eyes and saw that Jax had decided to masturbate right in front of her. Semen shot from his thick, heavily veined cock in seemingly endless spurts, covering both Sissy and Blinky. It was the first time Sissy had ever seen a man come, and it terrified her.

"You filthy pig," Blinky screamed, leaping up when he realized what was splashing atop him.

Jax's booming laugh echoed once more as he zipped himself back up. Then his smile vanished, and he stepped forward to clout Blinky square on the chest with a vicious punch. The little man slammed into the wall, opening up a long fissure in it, before he slid to the floor, moving as slowly as spilled glue."

"Don't ever raise your voice to me," the brute growled. "And I sure as hell don't want no name-calling from you, neither," he added. "Now get up."

Jax lifted up the wheezing form of Blinky and brought the unlucky creature to his feet. "Smile, mother-fucker!" he said. "I want to see that y'all still got your sense of humor."

The giant patted the smaller man contemptuously on the cheek and then turned to get a crusty-feeling robe, which he draped roughly about Sissy. "Let's go, Blondie," said Jax. "The boss is going to give you a *real* workout."

Chapter Twelve

After Foster and Hammer had run off, and Jerry had departed to fetch the Wolfmobile, Tiny was left alone with the drag queen. Tiny could name a dozen other creatures he'd *rather* be with. Poisonous adders, a mass murderer, an IRS representative, or even a Hari Krishna monk—anything was better than this creature in rouge and a sequined dress who was batting false eyelashes as if trying to send Morse code.

"My, my," the queen gushed, sending a whiff of ghastly breath into Tiny's face. "I don't see a single streak of gray in that beard. It must get a *lot* of exercise. Has someone been sitting on it often?"

The bounty hunter, for one of the rare times in his life, was at a loss for words.

"You better be nice to me," the queen insisted. "You just chased away my date for the night."

"Your date—what was his name?" Tiny asked, bravely trying to maintain a professional attitude, even though his cheeks burned a bright pink. Two leggy young girls sashayed past Tiny, giggling, further exasperating him.

"Look," said Tiny, going for broke. "I don't like you, and I don't want to talk with you. But I've got a fifty-dollar bill in my wallet for you if you know the guy's name; another two if you know where he lives."

The drag queen's voice went down three octaves.

"His name is . . . wait a second! Let me see the color of your money, sweetie."

Tiny reeled in his chain wallet like a fisherman hauling in a trout. He unsnapped it and took out a thick slab of hundreds, fifties, and twenties. The queen was nearly salivating. "Put up or shut up," Tiny growled. "Name and address."

"He goes by the name of Cooter." The queen made effeminate gestures while speaking. "I really don't know his last name, but I doubt he ever uses it much anyway. His address is on Pierce Street headed north. I don't have the exact address, but there's no way you can miss it. Some black folks live with Cooter there, and they put a *white* jockey out on their lawn."

"A jockey?" Tiny seemed puzzled. "Oh, I get it. One of them awful garden statues."

The bounty hunter forked over the gab money. The queen grabbed it and stuffed it down her bosom. "Nice doing business with you," she gushed. "Sure you don't want me to throw you something on the side?"

Tiny's face wrinkled with distaste, and Jerry, who had rejoined the big man, looked dangerously close to rapping the queen in the mouth.

"Calm down, Jerry!" Tiny commanded. "Let's go help Foster and Hammer!"

Chapter Thirteen

When Hammer saw Foster disappear into the driveway of the old brick house in pursuit of one of Sissy's
abductors, the quiet man silently cursed the writer's
lack of smarts. Tiny was right, Hammer thought to
himself as he closed in on the building. "Foster is a
man who does and says what he thinks," the bounty
hunter liked to say. "Unfortunately, he never thinks."

Hammer reached the lawn just as the report of Foster's Browning 9 mm sounded inside. Long years of
bounty hunting with Tiny had taught Hammer the
value of taking time to think before acting. The quiet
man was like a professional athlete who has been
around the league a long time but still delivers a superstar performance. He knew how to pace himself as well
as how to call on all his experience, to explode in a
mighty effort only when necessary. Just as he didn't
waste words, the big-shouldered man never made a
foolish or unnecessary move.

Hammer paused in front of a heavy white statue, not
taking the time to note what it was. He coiled himself
like a muscular cobra preparing to strike and burst into
the doorway with gun drawn. His preparation paid off.

Inside the entranceway, Hammer had little time to
take in the entire situation. All he saw as he moved
into the opening was the man he'd been chasing, bending slightly over the bloody form of Foster, setting

himself to plunge a knife downward into the unconscious figure.

Seeing Hammer, the fugitive dropped the knife and lowered his hand to his belt, hauling out a small nickel-plated handgun. But Hammer's gun was already on target. "Ho!" cried the quiet man, as if ordering a balky horse to stop.

But the other man brought the gun up, and Hammer squeezed the trigger of his weapon. Fired point-blank, two quick shots thudded into the man's body. His eyes flashed wide in a look of surprise that would remain until a mortician closed them. His gun went off as he sprawled backward against the stairs, losing itself a foot from Hammer's head. The quiet man reflexively pumped yet another bullet into the corpse.

Hammer bent to help Foster just as two more men slammed low into the entrance. The quiet man leveled his gun and then pocketed it upon seeing Tiny and Jerry crouching before him.

"Oh, shit!" Tiny yelled, seeing the spreading puddle of sticky blood all around the writer and a dead jaguar at his feet. "They got Foster."

But Jerry knelt quickly and put his head to the writer's chest. "He's breathing." The singer, a hunter in his youth, looked carefully at Foster and the big cat. "All right," he said, giving a low whistle of relief. "All this red shit belongs to the cat. Foster's Browning put a slug through its heart you can stick your arm through."

"He going to be all right?" Tiny asked.

"Well, it looks like he's taken a couple of deep claw strokes through his arms and chest. He'll need treatment and a tetanus shot, of course. And he might have some internal injuries, too. It appears to me like this big sucker done stove in Foster's ribs."

Tiny looked over the situation and then barked out orders without realizing that he was taking over as usual. "All right, Jerry! You get on the mobile phone and call an ambulance and the law. The Wolfmobile's right outside. Make sure Sidney doesn't tear your head off when you go in."

"Thanks, Tiny," Jerry answered, chuckling. "Be a hell of a way to go."

"Hammer!" Tiny continued. "You stay here with Foster till the meat wagon comes. I'm going to scout out this place to see what else is about. Cover me."

Hammer nodded but as usual gave no reply.

"Don't you talk back to me!" Tiny grinned, shifting his .357 into his southpaw shooting hand. A door to the right of the stairs was open, revealing some sort of storehouse. Boxes and packing crates were everywhere. Once someone's apartment, it served now as a catchall of clutter. The bounty hunter moved quickly and methodically about the room but saw no sign of life.

"Nothing doing there," he grunted to Hammer when he came back out into the entranceway. "Guess I'll invite myself upstairs." He paused, waiting until Jerry returned.

"I took care of everything," Jerry whispered as they went upstairs.

"I already knew that, Jerry." Tiny chuckled. "When ain't you taking care of things?"

But the bounty hunter's mirth ceased when he reached the last creaky stairs before the door. Tiny saw that the dead man downstairs had left the door open. He went in with all due caution, followed by Jerry.

A kitchen was the first room they entered. The stench of spoiled meat greeted them. "It's from that crate over there," Jerry said. "Smells like chicken."

"Yeah," Tiny agreed. "Probably fed that jaguar lots of backs and necks."

Through the closed kitchen door opposite the entrance, the bounty hunter and singer pushed inside to a huge chamber. Two rooms apparently had been converted into a single hall.

"Good Christ!" Jerry said, looking about. "Is someone kinky or what?"

The most obvious item in the room was a long marble altar, which by the Greek letters inscribed in its center had once reposed in a church. A long black bullwhip sat upon a linen cloth atop the altar, along with beeswax candles. The walls were hung with dozens of women's undergarments, many of them bloody, and with Polaroid photos of dozens of nude females, ranging in age from five to perhaps fifty.

"This is sick!" Tiny said, ripping down a photo of a child and tearing it to bits.

Jerry had moved over to a table upon which reposed a gold chalice and a raggedy doll. "Good Christ!" Jerry ejaculated. "Take a gander at this, Tiny."

The bounty hunter approached the singer, aware now of sirens in the distance and of how someone had painted every window black to match the somber ebony shade of the walls. "What you got?"

Jerry held up the raggedy doll for the bounty hunter to see. Tiny's mouth dropped as he beheld the doll, obviously homemade, which had a black beard, tattooed arms, and a vest very much like his own.

"Jesus. The damn thing looks like me."

"It is you," Jerry responded, showing uncharacteristic fear in his voice. "Don't you know what this is, brother?"

"Yeah, it's a doll."

"Not an ordinary doll, Tiny, not an ordinary doll. This here is a voodoo doll."

"Voodoo!"

"Yep, see the needle they stuck through its heart? It means only one thing—someone's got you marked for death."

Chapter Fourteen

After the oral attack on her person, Sissy was blind-folded and led into a car that still had the smell of newness about it. A hand twisted her wrist savagely and pushed her down in the back seat to make her invisible from the street.

"Lay there and don't get up!" said a voice she recognized as Blinky's, now trying to regain some of the manhood lost when Jax spurted semen all over him.

The ride began with sounds of the inner city—honking cars, squealing brakes, and shouts in the night—and ended after two hours in some serene country site. When she was pulled out of the car this time, Sissy felt a seashell-paved driveway under her feet.

Once they were inside the house, Sissy's blindfold was removed, and she was treated to a sight far more opulent than anything she'd imagined. The room had once served as a ballroom, and a heavy crystal chandelier hung down from the ceiling, featuring ornate glass like frosted icicles. A glowing fire was licking hungrily at scented wood in a fireplace decorated with white marble and ornate tile. The floor was elaborately polished wood held together by wooden pegs instead of nails, and the furniture looked as if it had been plucked out of the Smithsonian Institution.

"Pretty fancy digs, huh?" Blinky asked Sissy, who

was trying to keep her face impassive. "This is a two-hundred-year-old plantation home."

As Sissy looked around at the half dozen oil portraits of long-dead distinguished residents of the home, a pert, smartly dressed blond woman in her late thirties entered the room.

"Come with me, my dear," cooed the blond. "My name is Mickey. It's my job to help you look pretty for your grand entrance."

Much like a caring aunt or adoring older sister, the blond led Sissy away from Jax and Blinky. Mickey's departing glance at them showed her utter contempt for both. It was a look cold enough to freeze mercury.

The two women proceeded down a long hall and then went into a sitting room featuring a spiral staircase that seemed to wend its way straight up. The room was furnished with carefully polished brass antiques.

"Do you see that clock?" Mickey asked, her voice taking on the tone of a tour guide.

"Yes," Sissy responded in a cracked voice, the first word she had uttered in days.

"Notice that it's stopped at exactly 11:45 P.M. Old Mrs. Navarre, the last owner of this plantation, died at that time a few Christmases ago. The clock has never been reset. It's an old Louisiana custom. My boss, who took over this place, must have had a sentimental bone or two left in his body."

"'Oh! So I'm in Louisiana." Sissy decided to trust her. "I knew I was somewhere in the South, but I wasn't certain exactly where."

"Yeah, honey. Yo sho' in de deepest paht of de Deep South." Mickey laughed, her voice a manufactured accent filled with hominy grits. "My room is upstairs. You've got to take the staircase to get there."

Mickey's room proved to be a boudoir elegant enough to be used as a movie set. A huge white elephant of a tub with gold faucets reposed in one section of the room, and in another part there was a Victorian high-backed bed covered with a priceless seventeenth-century handmade quilt that took Sissy's breath away.

"We'll just get you all nice and clean, sweetheart," Mickey cooed. "And then we'll take a nice nap for a couple of hours to rest you up."

"Oh, thanks," said Sissy, again responding to the woman's apparent kindness after days of being subjected to Jax's mistreatment.

"No need to thank me," said Mickey. "Not in *words,* anyway."

Sissy's head shot up. There was a tone in Mickey's voice that had not been there previously. The woman's blue eyes had turned cold under her shag-cut frosted blond hair, and she looked different now to Sissy. Much different, cold and cruel, as her thin lips parted to show the tip of a sensual red tongue.

Mickey stepped forward and took hold of Sissy's robe right below the collar. With a sudden jerk she tore the garment clear down to Sissy's navel. The blond looked into Sissy's eyes and then gazed with unconcealed lust at the girl's white breasts, which showed clearly through the ripped fabric.

Without another word, Mickey tugged quickly at her own silky Halston dress and pulled it over her head. All she had on now were black lace bikini briefs and a lacy black bra. A quick couple of movements, and soon these two garments landed in small puddles on the floor.

Sissy had never seen another woman completely nude. Her high school in St. Jo had insisted that modesty be kept, and so private showers had been provided for each girl during gym class. Unconsciously, her glance dropped to Mickey's dark-colored nipples, which even as she looked were hardening into arrow tips. Below a still trim stomach showing neither scar nor blemish lay a pubic patch lighter even than Sissy's fair cornsilk.

Mickey continued to look at Sissy's breasts with unabashed lust. Stepping forward once again, she lifted a trim leg and hooked Sissy's torn robe with a rose-painted toe, tearing it downward the rest of the way.

"Come, Sissy, darling," Mickey urged, her voice husky and her breath coming hard. "I'll draw our bath, and we'll scrub each other clean as pie. Afterwards, we'll play a little game. You'll still be a virgin when the boss gets you in a few hours, but only technically.

"Now," she continued, her eyes cold as crystals, "will you get your ass into the tub, or shall I make you get in?"

Chapter Fifteen

Nightfall found Hammer and Tiny visiting Foster Foster in a semiprivate room at the Medical Center of New Orleans on Saint Charles Avenue. Jerry's diagnosis had turned out to be right on the money. Foster had suffered some painful lacerations and bruised ribs—though no breaks—and was scheduled for release the next morning after a night of observation.

"Hey, where's Jerry?" Foster asked suddenly after Tiny and Hammer exchanged greetings with him.

"Don't worry yourself to death," Tiny growled. "He'll be here. The guy you ought to be talking to is Hammer, here. He's the one that helped you keep your topknot intact. That scumbag in that house was ready to give you a haircut from the *inside* of your head out."

"Hey!" protested the writer, shaking the quiet man's hand. "Don't think I'm not grateful, Tiny. But don't tell me I'm supposed to have a conversation with him. My God, I don't think Hammer has uttered a dozen sentences in his life."

Suddenly an orderly entered, wheeling in a shiny cart covered with a white cloth. "That's funny," Foster said, "they already brought me a meal tonight."

The orderly came over to the side of the bed. "Not like this meal, they ain't!" he chortled, sweeping aside the cloth to reveal a bucket of the láte colonel's finest crunchy chicken and two six packs of Michelob.

Foster did two double-takes as he looked over at the beer first and then the "orderly."

"Jerry!" the writer cried. "How the hell did you pull *this* stunt off?"

"Professional secret, old man!" Jerry sniffed. "Now, are you boys going to dive into the goodies or do I have to polish them off myself?"

Neither Foster, Hammer, nor Tiny ever required a second invitation when it came to eating or drinking, but Foster stopped himself in the middle of a drumstick and called across the room to where a grizzled old-timer was sitting up in bed thumbing through a scholarly journal.

"Hey, Boudin!" the writer shouted across the room. "Put down that book and come join us. I forgot my manners."

The man flashed a smile wide as a Louisiana rainbow across his bristly, suntanned face. He was in his fifties or sixties, judging by the look of him, with a hide so tough even a shark would spit him back out. When he opened his mouth, one expected him to talk in an illiterate fashion, but instead he sounded like a college professor with a musical Cajun accent.

"Very cordial of you, Foster, if I may say so." Boudin scrambled out of bed to stroll over with a chair in his hand. "These, I take it, are the friends you've told me about all day?"

When Foster nodded and introduced his three cronies, the Cajun politely bowed his head to each in turn, looking a bit ridiculous from a back view since his bare keister flashed through his hospital gown.

"Anthony Crozat is my name, gentlemen, but everyone knows me by my AKA, which happens to be Boudin. They called me that after I won a boudin-eating contest up in Donaldsonville one day. Chomped down thirty of those hot sausages in five minutes, I did."

Tiny and his companions hoisted themselves up to pump hands with the strange little man whose humorous good nature was contagious. The bounty hunter looked oddly at his hand after shaking; the skinny guy had a grip like a pit bull's.

"Uh, if you don't mind my asking," Tiny growled, "what is it you do for a living? That's some strength you got in those wrists of yourn."

"Oh, I do a little of this, a little of that. Guide mostly, I guess. Trap in one season, collect oysters in another, and shoe horses whenever I'm needed."

"You sure don't talk like a swamp rat," Jerry said, twisting off a beer cap and handing the newcomer a brew.

"No, that I don't. I taught English almost twenty years at Tulane University here in New Orleans, but I hated every minute of it. Every free moment I had would find me scampering off to the bayou country to hunt and fish. It took me a long time, but finally something snapped, and I departed for good one June."

"Are you happier now?" Jerry asked.

"Do I look sad?" Boudin quipped. "I do what I want, when I want. No, my only regret is that I didn't leave teaching about nineteen years sooner."

"What are you in the hospital for?" Tiny asked. "You look healthy as a horse."

"I am, but the young bedmate I was with two weeks ago apparently didn't enjoy similar health."

"You got the clap?" Tiny chortled.

"Unfortunately, yes." Boudin giggled. "With slight complications due to a reaction I had to the medication. I can't wait until I'm released in the morning."

Tiny took a thoughtful swallow of beer, draining half the bottle. "You say you're a guide?"

"A damn good one."

"You doing anything special tomorrow?"

"Definitely." Boudin grinned. "I can tell by the tone of your voice that you are offering me a position. I accept."

"Hey, not so fast," Tiny said. "Sure, you got a job, but you ain't heard what it is yet. You might get your ass shot up with a lot more than just penicillin."

"I live my life the way I want, Tiny. I'll die the same way. All I ask is a sailing ship and a star to steer her by."

"Huh?"

"In other words, my dear fellow, it doesn't take much to keep me happy. Boredom is the only thing I hate. A little danger now and then keeps the blood from coagulating. A man cannot live forever, though I'll try; and dying holds no terror for me. Do we have a deal?"

"We do," Tiny said, extending his paw. "Consider yourself one of the boys as of now."

The beer disappeared fast, but the stories continued to flow during the two-hour session. A nurse looked in from time to time, puzzled by the hearty masculine laughter roaring out into the hall and unaware of the empty bottles Hammer had hidden under the bed. Tiny had just finished telling a tale about being on *this* side of the law and had launched into one about being on the other side.

"There was this time in St. Jo when Jerry and me was flat busted and down, which wasn't too unusual in them days," recalled Tiny. "So's I get it into my head that we're goin' to make a little bank withdrawal without making a deposit first. I picked out this old bank, which is right next door to a confectionery store which was recently closed down. I figure this job's a cinch since the store and the bank's got this big thick wall in common. We just punch a hole in the wall neater than shit and scoop out the money—right?

"But like the man says, anything that *can* go wrong is *gonna* go wrong. We break into the old store through an unlocked window and scope out the situation. Jerry had gone into the bank that day and knew exactly where the safe was hid, so's we started busting into the wall. Well, that wall turns out to be about as thick as Foster's head; and after one solid night of digging and picking, we still ain't managed to get inside. Well, we see it's starting to get light out, so *we* decide to light out, too.

"We come back the next night, only we got a slight problem. Me and Jerry had gotten together about 3 P.M. to discuss the job, and he'd brought this bottle of red worm tequila with him. Before you know it, we're tighter than a Scottish pawnbroker, but we decide to go ahead with the job anyway. To top matters off, I managed to catch me a bodacious case of the flu, and I was both shitting and sneezing like a son of a bitch. I mean, you talk about being sore!

"Well, once more we work through the night, and this time the work goes a lot faster because Jerry's had the foresight to bring along a *second* bottle of tequila. So I mean, there I am, digging and sneezing and shitting and laughing like hell all night long, like me and Jerry was *supposed* to be in a broken-down candy store at midnight trying to rob us a bank.

"To get to the heart of the matter, we finally manage to bust into the place about 5 A.M., but by then we're so pooped and shitfaced we figure that it's time to take a little rest. Bam! The next thing you know it's 9 A.M., and Jerry's shaking my arm off, trying to wake me up. Well, we start collecting bag after bag of money, trying to get the hell out with about four sacks apiece. But then my goddamn stomach gets the best of me, and if I don't go on the floor, I'm goin' to soil my pants. So I drop my drawers, and you never saw such a bad case of Hershey squirts."

"I mean it was *ba-ad*," Jerry interrupted. "So what happens is my stomach is none too steady after our drinking bout, and I end up losing my cookies after taking one whiff of Tiny."

"And you know what happens when one guy throws up," Tiny continued. "Right away I'm hunched there with my pants down, and then I'm losing a load front and back. There ain't no toilet paper in there, of course, so's I grab the next best thing, which happens to be a pile of hundred-dollar bills. But no sooner do I start rubbing poor Ben Franklin's snout up my backside than I get this powerful urge to sneeze."

"I see he's goin' to sneeze," Jerry interrupted, "so's I grab him by the nose. I mean, the bank's already open now, and we can hear voices outside clear as day."

"But when a sneeze wants to come out, it's going to come out," Tiny continued, "and I let loose this whooper, which goes off like a gunshot in the vault. I mean, you could hear a pin drop outside the vault. Everyone stopped talking, and then I could hear someone messin' with the combination lock on the safe. In about ten seconds, the manager or the security guard or both are going to be stepping in our shit!"

"Literally," Jerry interrupted again. "So's we grab our picks and shovels to book out the hole in the wall."

"Only at better than three hundred pounds, I don't squeeze quite as easily through no hole," said Tiny. "Jerry's on the other side yelling 'Come on, you fat motherfucker!' whilst he's pulling on my arms till I think they're going to fall off. Finally, I get inside the candy store just as the safe door opens up. With no time to lose, me and Jerry just grab the pick and shovel with our fingerprints on them and leave behind eight sacks of money as we book out the window to our car."

"I'd hate to have been you guys," Boudin said, holding his sides from laughing so hard.

"You'd hate to have been us?" Tiny asked. "Hell, I

was feeling sorry for whoever they was goin' to make wash off all them hundred-dollar bills."

Tiny looked up to see a stern, prune-faced nurse in the doorway. She had been listening to every word.

"Gentlemen," said Tiny. "I got a feeling me, Jer, and Hammer is being 86'ed. We'll see you in the morning, as soon as they kick you both out."

"Tomorrow it is," said Boudin, moving off toward his bed. "I'll just have to stop at my cabin south of here to pick up my gear and to collect a few of my traplines, if you don't mind."

"Done!" boomed Tiny.

"By the way," Boudin mused, "who exactly are we after, and what has he done?"

"A no-good pimp and killer that kidnaped my seventeen-year-old niece," Tiny growled, slapping his black hat atop his head. "They call him the Jaguar."

Boudin blanched under his tan, and he made a face as if he suddenly were going to become ill. "Ooh," he grunted, as if Tiny had slugged him in the belly.

"You know him?" Tiny demanded, as the head nurse ushered him out into the corridor.

"You might say that," Boudin responded weakly, easing himself into bed. "He's my son."

Chapter Sixteen

Sissy sat disconsolately on the edge of Mickey's bed, feeling too debased even to shed tears. She took a sideward glance at Mickey, lying alongside her in a sheer negligee, an unfiltered cigarette jammed between her lips.

The older woman eyed the girl narrowly. "Come on, Sissy," she said. "Own up to it. You did enjoy what we did, didn't you?"

Sissy turned to Mickey, a look of revulsion on her pretty features. "When my Uncle Tiny comes for me—and you'd better believe he'll find me—I'm going to have him tear your heart right out of your chest."

Mickey laughed cruelly and took another long drag of smoke. "The trouble with this new generation is that you kids aren't into experimentation. I like it any way I can get it. Makes no difference to me. Boys, men, girls . . ."

"Pigs, dogs, goats!" Sissy snarled. "Yeah, I can tell, *you'd* fuck anything."

"Yes, my dear," Mickey said in a tone that showed that Sissy was getting to her. "And with the aid of a few little gadgets, I've also had sex with *you*. Not inside you, I know. That's for the boss's pleasure. But I've had enough to keep me satisfied for a couple of hours."

The woman glanced over at her watch on the night

table. "My, it's nearly time for our little meeting with the boss. How time flies when one's having sugar."

Mickey lifted her trim legs off the bed and strolled over to a closet to rummage through a wardrobe of expensive outfits that could have covered fifty women. Mickey slipped off the filmy negligee and ran her fingers up and down her body, eyes reduced to slits as she caressed her own skin. Sissy looked almost in wonderment at the woman's smooth body, flawed only by an almost comical red blemish on her backside. Suddenly the phone rang; Mickey picked it up on the second ring.

"Yes, we're nearly ready," she cooed. "Twenty minutes? You've got it, Boss."

Mickey brought her nude body right next to Sissy's and yanked the girl upright by the hair. She placed the captive's face a half inch from her left breast. "Lick it!" she said.

Sissy's instinct was to take one hardening nipple and bite it clear off, but she did not do so, knowing that death would follow instantly. Hesitantly, the girl put out her tongue, flicked at the arrowlike hardness once, and then pulled her tongue in again.

"No," Mickey snarled. "If you can't do it right up here, let's see what you can do down there." The woman knocked the unclothed girl onto her knees and by applying cruel pressure to the back of Sissy's head forced her face into the sparse blond hair. "Lick me," she commanded. "Put your tongue up me."

With salty tears blinding her eyes, Sissy hesitantly obeyed. Mickey grabbed the girl's head with both hands, moaning with pleasure. "Yes, yes, yes!" she cried over and over, rotating her hips. For nearly three minutes, Mickey ground her pubic patch into Sissy's face, feeling the pleasure of the girl's unwilling tongue deep within her. Suddenly, Mickey moaned and writhed spasmodically, filling the air with profanities.

Her face turned radiant, Mickey dropped onto the

floor beside Sissy and tried to kiss the girl softly on the lips. Sissy turned away, and the kiss brushed coldly upon her cheek.

"Suit yourself," Mickey said. "It's time for a quick shower, my dear. It won't do at all for the boss to kiss you while your lips are full of my juices. God knows, he knows their taste well enough by now."

Chapter Seventeen

The Wolfmobile pulled up to the outpatient exit of the medical center at 9 A.M. the morning after Tiny's visit. Foster and Boudin were already outside awaiting them. Foster had on his usual motley assortment of clothes, topped by his Yankee batting helmet, while Boudin looked every inch the trapper in his chamois shirt with muskrat-fur vest.

Sidney came right up to Boudin and licked his hand when the old man clambered aboard. Tiny pumped the old man's hand and bopped Foster alongside the helmet till his ears rang by way of greeting. "God damn, Boudin!" Tiny said. "I ain't never seen Sidney go for a stranger like that. Guess I won't need no better a character reference."

"Morning, boys," said Foster. "Bet you were all lost without me."

"Oh yeah," Jerry responded drily. "We been sitting here crying in our mush 'cause we got nobody to pick on and blame stuff on."

"These two boys always get along so well?" asked Boudin, handing a homemade map with directions to his cabin over to Hammer at the wheel.

"You got it," Tiny told him. "Foster and Jerry are one another's natural enemies, just like the spider and the fly. You see, me and Jerry and Foster all grew up together, got in trouble together, and whatnot. Only

Foster started turning weird at an early age, and we sort of drifted apart."

"Yeah," Jerry added. "We was all getting in trouble, but Foster never did get caught. And anything *he* did, me and Tiny got blamed for."

"Like what?" Boudin asked.

"Oh, you name it and Foster done it," Tiny told him. "There was the time Foster broke into the school cafeteria and mixed in a bag of cement base with the instant potatoes. *I* got suspended three days for that stunt, and I wasn't even there. But do you think old Foster here would be a hero and own up to the fact? Nope! And there wasn't a damn thing I could do about it because of our code against squealing. Well, almost nothing I could do about it."

"Yeah," Foster added sourly. "You tied me naked to a post in the girls' gym."

"That's right." Tiny chuckled, but then his grin faded. "Only *that* stunt got me suspended for two *weeks!*"

"I remember the time Foster snuck into the biology lab and filled a bunch of them dissecting frogs with ketchup packed in plastic bags," said Jerry. "We was in the class at the time, too, and all these kids started popping open them frogs and gagging 'cause they thought it was real blood. Old Mr. Rudewicz blamed us for the stunt and made us catch him thirty live frogs by the next day."

"Did you ever pay back Foster for that deed?" Boudin asked.

"I'll say." Jerry giggled. "Paybacks are standard procedure in this outfit. You can play a joke on anyone you like, but you got to be prepared to pay. After Foster pulled off that shit in the biology lab, me and Tiny stuck a frog in his lunch pail."

"That doesn't sound so bad."

"We put the bugger in his *thermos,*" Jerry continued, "and then snuck over to watch Foster gulp it down. He was sitting with Sue Ellen Hirsch, one of the foxiest girls in all Missouri, and she nearly puked on the spot when Foster jumped up and pulled that green hopper out of his mouth. She thought he done it on purpose just to aggravate her."

"I'd forgotten about that," Foster said sourly. "Then I had to put up with these two clowns asking me if I had a frog in my throat for the next two weeks each time they ran into me."

"Anyway," Tiny continued, "after me and Jerry got expelled from high school, Foster stayed in and went on to college for more book learning. We did anything you can think of that was illegal for a while, until our probation officer found out that Jerry could pick and sing. As luck would have it, the officer's brother had need for someone to play in his band in Nashville. Afore you know it, Jerry was playing for some of the biggest names in country music inside of two years."

"Yeah," Foster interrupted, "and getting drummed out of every band he was in for fucking up. Like one time he was supposed to play at the Grand Ole Opry but got too shitfaced to go on. The singer punished him by not letting Jerry play that night, but that didn't stop him, not by a long shot. He stayed quietly in the wings until the grand finale song, which was 'Ghost Riders in the Sky,' when he decided to run out on stage wearing a bedsheet. He was flapping his arms and going 'whoo, whoo, whoo' until the whole place was in stitches. The band leader didn't think it was too funny, though. He busted his guitar over Jerry's head, which started a near riot at the Opry."

"Yeah," Tiny recalled, "and then there was the time he was on tour with some bitchy singer or another, and he ended up sleeping with her. Well, one night after a performance, Jerry was told that he'd have to stay in his room alone that night because her husband was coming up for a visit."

"What did you do to her?" Boudin asked, spell-bound by the stories.

"I snuck up to her room afore her and her old man came in and got to fixing the place up for his arrival. I messed up all the sheets and blankets, then on the bed I left this new condom, which I stretched and twisted to make it look used."

"I'll bet you really got in trouble for that," Boudin said.

"Not immediately." Jerry chuckled. "I had snuck into our road manager's room first and stole his shoes and suit, which had a bunch of business cards inside."

"Don't tell me you left his clothes in her closet?" Boudin seemed horrified at the thought.

"You got it," Jerry said. "The singer and her husband had no sooner walked into the room than in busted the road manager without knocking. He was all upset about his clothes being gone, but he never got a chance to say anything before the old boy cold-cocked him for supposedly making it with his wife."

"What about Hammer?" Boudin laughed, pointing to the quiet man driving them south along the Great River Road. "Did he grow up with you all?"

"No," said Tiny. "What happened is that Jerry got into singing, and Foster here got into writing articles for magazines, so I kind of drifted around the country after a judge ordered me out of Missouri for fucking up once too often. I joined a bike gang and ended up being national president. Hammer was in the club, and me and him just hit it right off. After I got into bounty hunting for a bail bondsman named Joey Hudson who hauled me out of jail in exchange for working for him, Hammer hired on as my assistant."

"He's sure talkative, isn't he?"

"You noticed that, did you?" Tiny laughed and then turned sober. "Hammer's pa caught his old lady dicking around one night. Shot her, the lover, and himself.

Hammer saw the whole thing and kind of went into shock. Wouldn't say a word for the longest time. He's come out of it OK but still don't talk much. When he does, though, everyone listens close 'cause he's got something important to say." The bounty hunter looked affectionately over at his silent partner. "Like now," said Tiny. "Hammer's motioning you over. He's got a question about your map."

The drive to Boudin's cabin off Bastian Bay took less than ninety minutes. The cabin was actually a charming two-bedroom affair in the Cajun style. Although a faded gray in color, the place was anything but dismal in aspect, with cypress shingles on the outside and a roof of corrugated metal. Although Boudin had electricity and running water, an outhouse stood a short walk away as a remembrance of times past.

"You must be hungry," Boudin said, showing off his Cajun hospitality.

The old man walked over to the woodpile and came back with the makings for a fire, which he spread over some five-pound rocks. "Jerry," the trapper said, "you've got the look of a woodsman about you. Would you mind getting a blaze started while I look to the meal?"

After Boudin had gone inside, Foster approached Tiny, speaking in a whisper. "I can't stand it any more," he said. "Aren't you going to ask Boudin about his son?"

"Nope," the bounty hunter answered. "I figure that when he's ready, he'll tell us."

After Jerry had started a roaring blaze and set up a blackened piece of animal hide to serve as heat reflector, Boudin came out with a crockery pot filled with roux—flour soaked in grease—which he set aside until the flames died down, leaving white charcoal over the red-hot rocks. "This stuff has to cook nice and slow,"

Boudin said. "Otherwise, it turns to a mess that looks and smells like a melted tire. You got to stir it while it cooks until it's the color of a bear's ass."

As the roux bubbled in the pot, Boudin handed round a jug of red wine, from which each man took a warm mouthful. When everyone had taken a swallow, Boudin screwed the top back on and wiped his mouth with the back of his hand.

The old trapper looked thoughtful as he stared down into the glowing rocks. "A long, long time ago," he began, "my son Revon used to sit here with me by a fire, just as you men do now. He was a handsome Cajun boy, eyes black as the night ocean, with hair to match and a smile that even then melted the hearts of all the girls. As you can tell," Boudin continued, managing a grin, "he looked like his mother, God have mercy on her."

"I take it Revon is the one everyone calls the Jaguar today," Foster commented.

Boudin nodded. "His mother, as I say, is dead. I heard that Rose died in the streets of Metairie, outside New Orleans, in a slum whorehouse where only those who wanted women totally wasted by either age, drink, or social disease ever ventured."

"Your son," encouraged Foster. "Do you believe his behavior today is directly affected by his mother's whoring?"

"That started him hating women, of that I am sure. He was accused of beating two girls when he was in high school. I was away during the day, teaching classes, and he used to skip school to bring his young girls here. He was not content with seducing them. Always he had to hurt them in some way. If he couldn't break their hearts, then he slapped them around. At least three girls were knocked up that I know about. I personally was forced to take two girls to an angel maker."

"An angel maker?" Tiny asked.

"An abortionist," Boudin informed him. "But even though Revon was bad in those days, you wouldn't actually call him evil. In fact, many nights I'd wake up to hear him crying his eyes out in bed. I tried to take him to a shrink, but he refused to go."

"What made him, as you say, evil?" Tiny asked, gaining the courage to speak from Boudin's openness.

"There was an armed robbery in a little town near here called Port Sulphur. The shopkeeper couldn't identify the robber, so he told the police that it was my son."

"You don't think he did it?" Foster asked.

"Absolutely not. My son may be a lot of things, but a liar he isn't. He swore to me that he didn't do it."

"Then why did he name him?"

"The shopkeeper's daughter was one of those girls my son had made pregnant. He hated him with a fury, and so did she. The night of the robbery, my son happened to be off in the woods to check on some traps. There was no one who could refute the store owner's story."

"How long did they send him up for?" Jerry asked.

"Two years. The shopkeeper said that he was robbed at gunpoint. Not only that, the guy said that he was robbed of $700. The judge made me honor-bound to make restitution."

"Two years in the slammer, huh?" Tiny said. "That really changed the kid?"

"Brutalized him even worse," Boudin explained. "There he met a lot of cutthroats who offered to set him up when he got out. Prison hardened him to the point of no return. His first day out of prison, there were two murders in Port Sulphur."

"The shopkeeper and his daughter?" Tiny asked.

"Right. Only this time Revon had an airtight alibi. The murders went unsolved."

"How did he get the name 'Jaguar'?" Hammer asked, causing his companions to look at him in amazement for showing such loquaciousness.

"Revon always loved animals as a kid, and he always had a way with them. Dogs, lizards, snakes, cats—you name it, he collected it and trained it. When he got out of prison, one of his girlfriends had purchased a pair of jaguars from some fly-by-night pet store. When they proved too much for her, he took them over. Jaguars aren't usually the kind of animal that will jump when a human gives orders. Even the Hollywood trainers shy away from using them. But, like I said, Revon has a way with animals. Those big cats of his will do anything he commands: come when called, roll over, or kill. It's all the same to them."

"How many does he have?" Jerry asked.

"He's bred at least six. I don't know for sure. We don't speak. He told me that he never wants to see me again. If I ever talk to the police, he's threatened to have me killed. He says that if I had been more of a man, my wife wouldn't have run around. He blames me for her infidelity and the ruination of his own life. He's what they call a bad seed."

"Then why are you going with us to track him?"

"I don't know exactly. It's something I've often thought about doing all on my own, perhaps as a way to assuage my guilt. There isn't a racket he isn't involved in. Drugs—he controls the whole operation, using one-time poachers who know the swamps like they know their names to haul in shit past snake-infested places where the law wouldn't dare go. Prostitution? He controls half the pimps in New Orleans and supplies young girls to rings all over the country. If he's not the biggest white slaver in the country, name me another man who is. Murder for hire? Name the victim; he'll name the price."

"Only one thing left for you to tell us," Tiny said. "How do we get to him?"

"I've got two or three good leads," Boudin replied. "Let me go into the house for some fixings for the pot to make us a community gumbo. Then we'll come up with a game plan."

Chapter Eighteen

With the point of Mickey's snub-nosed gun in her ribs, Sissy wasn't about to cause a scene as she left the boudoir to meet the Jaguar. Instead of blindly listening to Mickey, she took in every detail of the great plantation house as they walked, looking for an escape route.

The slave-built manor was truly magnificent, and under different circumstances Sissy would have been enthralled. Every brick and tile had been made on the premises, and the elaborate hand-carved wooden trimmings had been manufactured in England and shipped at great cost. As they walked, Sissy peered into open rooms with ceilings of twenty feet or more and massive Gothic-style doors pulled back. Every room, it seemed, had its own fireplace, and all the windows were beautifully latticed. Through the windows Sissy had a view of a great expanse of lawn and giant oaks in the distance. What she would give to be able to make one desperate dash across that lawn to freedom. But a glance at Mickey's stern, unyielding face and the equally foreboding gun in her hand warned Sissy that any move out of the ordinary meant certain death.

At the end of the hall Sissy was led into yet another great room furnished with rather gaudy Victorian period furniture, with red the dominant color. On the walls were the heads of several American big-game animals:

cougar, mountain goat, bighorn sheep, and grizzly bear. A taxidermist had caught the predatory cougar and grizzly in all their ferocity, and they looked ready to leap off the wall on command.

But it wasn't the furnishings that held Sissy's attention. Her blue eyes were transfixed by a brace of jaguars lying on either side of a thronelike chair upon which sat the most swashbuckling-looking man she had ever laid eyes upon. In another time and place, Sissy knew that this was a man who might captivate her heart. His eyes were raven-black, and his black hair cascaded in soft curls along his neck. But there was nothing in the man to suggest a similar softness. His eyes showed not even a glimmer of light as his lips opened in a mechanical smile that displayed even white teeth.

A noise sounded behind Sissy, and she turned with a shudder as six fierce-looking men entered the room. Two of them she recognized immediately as Blinky and Jax: out of some primitive survival instinct, she made a grab for Mickey's gun, which her captor quickly lifted out of her reach.

"I see we have more than just these two cats in the room," said the man in a melodic voice. "Allow me to introduce myself. The name is Revon Crozat. You, I take it, are Sissy."

The blond girl looked defiantly over at Revon and his jaguars. She did not return his smile. All the soft-spoken words in the world could not make her forget that this man was directly responsible for the debasement she had suffered the last few days.

"I have an uncle," was all Sissy would say, "who is going to tear your heart out of your chest and kick it into the nearest sewer."

"Ah, yes, your bounty-hunting relative. My contacts have him under surveillance already. He does not trouble me. In fact, since you are so sure of what he would do with my heart, given the chance, maybe I will serve you his on a platter when we vanquish him."

Sissy looked her foe in the eye and then shot him her middle finger.

"I like that spirit in my women. No doubt yours is a result of your virginity. You just haven't met the right man yet."

"And I take it that the right man is supposed to be you?" Sissy asked.

"Correct." Revon laughed, displaying his ivory teeth. The man they called the Jaguar flicked a small black riding whip against his boot, as if keeping time to music. He was clad entirely in black, from an open-neck silk shirt to boots that fit snugly beneath a pair of expensive pants.

When Sissy failed to respond, the Jaguar continued his spiel, obviously enjoying himself at the girl's expense. "To be fair, my dear, I'll give you a choice. Take your sexual awakening at my hands or at the pleasure of any other person in this room."

Sissy looked about in confusion. The half dozen men in the room all looked unwashed and thuggish. Each seemed capable of ripping her in two during the sexual act. No relief was in sight when Sissy's eyes darted upon Mickey, who stood seductively, glaring back at her, a wet tongue protruding through her lips.

"Some choice," said Sissy. "Sex with a barbarian like you or hyenas like them."

"I do not appreciate your name-calling," the Jaguar said, his eyes beginning to smolder. "When the mouse is in a predator's mouth, it should not make bold to squeak."

Sissy looked anxiously into her captor's face. The anger in his voice had communicated itself to the big cats, and they were on their feet now, straining at the leash.

"Yes, my dear," Revon said, working on Sissy's

obvious fear. "If you prefer that none of *us* enjoy you, perhaps you would rather leave this world a martyr."

Sissy peered into the man's dark eyes. No mercy showed anywhere on that handsome face. If she was going to act, it had better be quickly.

"I don't know why you'd have any use for me any longer," Sissy said, trying to keep her voice defiant but failing slightly.

"What do you mean?"

"I'm not exactly undamaged goods anymore."

"I don't understand."

"Ask your little army about what they've been doing to me. Ask Blinky there, and Jax, and Mickey."

The three figures blanched when they heard their names. Jax angrily took a step toward Sissy, but a barked command from Revon froze him in his tracks.

"Leave her alone!" Revon commanded, looking at each culprit in turn. "What truth is there in what she speaks?"

The trio began chattering at once, each offering frightened denials. The cowardly Blinky was in tears, and the other two had lost their insolent bearing.

With the tables turning slightly in her favor, Sissy spoke to the Jaguar in her sauciest manner. "Would you like proof?"

"You had better have proof," Revon asserted, a grim smile on his handsome features. "If you do, my cats will feast upon them. If you lie, however, it is you who will die."

Chapter Nineteen

For a few minutes all thought of the manhunt was gone as Tiny and his men feasted on gumbo as dark and thick as Minnesota farmland. Inside the cast-iron pot was a rich mixture of oysters, shrimp, sea bass, finfish, and crabs, complemented by enough crawdads to create a meal fit for a king. And Tiny did look somewhat like a king at that moment, propping up his butt on a cypress stump, surrounded by loyal foot soldiers, a look of utter contentment on his face as he spooned in bite after bite. Also looking blissful was Sidney, who was catching tidbits tossed to him every minute or so by his masters.

During the first three or four bowls of gumbo, each man was silent. Even Foster, for once, had put a cinch on his yapper. When the bounty hunter and his crew were sated, Boudin looked into the empty pot with amazement.

"You know," Boudin marveled as he scraped out the dregs for a few last bites, "once I fed twenty of my neighbors on a pot of gumbo this size. In all my life I have never seen anyone put away more food."

"Oh shit!" Tiny said repentantly. "Does this mean you ain't going to give us no dessert?"

Boudin laughed and marched into the cabin, emerging with an armload of cans. He tossed a small can of peaches at each of the guests but declined to take one for himself.

The five hunters looked like mountain men who have just gorged themselves after a successful buffalo hunt. Boudin was first to break the silence. "I take it you've been in this bounty-hunting business for quite a spell, Tiny?"

The big man nodded. "Going on four years now by my count."

"How many men have you brought back?"

"Almost four hundred," Tiny said matter of factly. "Why?"

"Oh, guess I was just sitting here wondering what was the toughest hunt you've ever been on."

"The toughest hunt? Hell, I know what was the hunt that made me the proudest, but it wasn't a man I was after."

"What was it?" Boudin asked, handing out toothpicks to all present except Tiny, whose teeth had long since departed in violent incidents, which he claimed made him the undisputed best at oral sex.

"A Rocky Mountain bighorn sheep," Tiny said. "Old Hammer here was with me on that one."

The quiet man nodded his head to back his partner's tale.

"For a couple of years," said Tiny, who needed only the smallest excuse to launch into a story, "I'd been submitting my name to the Idaho fish and gamers to put into their annual lottery. Well, finally, last year it came through. I made all the arrangements with an outfitter, and on the opening day of hunting season, me and Hammer drove from L.A. to Idaho in a motor home."

"The Wolfmobile?" Boudin asked.

"No, some other one which got wrecked in Arizonee when I rammed a couple of good old boys in their Ramcharger after they'd tried to air-condition us with shotgun pellets. Anyhow, we get to Salmon, Idaho, in the middle of nowhere, and that's as far as we could go with the motor home. When you get to the Idaho primitive area, you got three ways to go: by plane, by foot, and on horseback. Now, I'm scared to death of even big planes, but walking and riding just never did excite this three-hundred-eighty-nine-pound frame of mine, though I'll do both when forced into it.

"So we go to this little air-taxi outfit outside of Salmon and charter us one of them little single-engine Cessna 172 jobbers. Well, I mean to tell you that if the ride didn't scare the shit out of you, nothing would. Plus the ride was as noisy as a son of a bitch; you had to shout just to talk. And even worse, we picked up a tail wind along the way, which sent that plane hopping like a fart in a bottle.

"You talk about scared, I was shitting green bricks. And then this old boy who was piloting us leans over to point out all the spots where people died in plane crashes, which didn't do much for *my* confidence, I'll tell you. But you talk about pretty! Why, that Idaho landscape was laid out just like a big green canopy. In places you couldn't even see the ground, just the tops of trees. And talk about game, I saw a whole slew of bighorns, elk, and even a goddamn mountain lion feasting on a dead deer. It was an experience you had to be there to believe.

"But after about forty-five minutes, just about when I was used to the feeling of my stomach jumping into my throat and falling down on my nuts, the pilot announced that we was ready to land. But you wouldn't believe how small the airstrip was we had to land on. Airstrip? Hell, it was just a dug-out trench in the forest that you'd have trouble parking a Cadillac on top of, let alone a plane. Anyhow, he slows the plane down to about sixty mph and then white-knuckles an oxbow curve to come swooping down at that strip like a hawk after a rat. Right then and there, I nearly lost the bacon and henfruit I'd scarfed down for breakfast, but that pilot set down that Cessna like he was setting good china on a table.

"The outfitter's waiting for us with a pack horse, and after we get down to his cabin to transfer gear, we start out after my bighorn sheep. Now, to tell you the truth, I didn't know much about Idaho before I got there. I had no idea the terrain was going to be so damn steep. I mean, there's only two ways you can go in those Salmon River Mountains: straight up or straight down. Plus, when you're standing there surrounded by mountains everywhere, you sort of feel like a fly in the middle of a jug, looking for a way out.

"Anyhow, we start chugging up ridge after ridge, and I'm sweating bullets, and so's Hammer. The outfitter, unfortunately, is this skinny little mother who can outwalk the legs off a coyote. But you know me—never quit something once I start it. For two days we walked and walked and walked, but we didn't see nothing with fur on it. You don't think a rifle and pack can get heavy, you just try walking twenty miles of uphill country some time.

"Anyhow, the third morning I wake up out of my pack, and I figure I got to still be dreaming. The biggest, most beautiful bighorn ram you ever want to see in your life is standing in some bushes looking back at me no more than eighty feet away. In the meantime, both Hammer and the outfitter are awake by this time, but they're keeping still as field mice. Real slow, an inch at a time, I reach for my rifle. But no sooner do I get my claws wrapped around the barrel, when the damn thing spooks and disappears into the brush quick as a cough.

"Instantly, the three of us are off. We leave the pack horse and our cache behind. All we take is our guns, ammo, and a belly pack of grub. Now that skinny old boy couldn't read a book, but he'd been well schooled in the art of the wilderness and could read a trail so good it amazed me. A busted twig, a clump of fur in a bramble, or a split rock told him as much as if a traffic cop was out there, pointing him on. to the ram. Ridge after ridge we went, while me and Hammer's tongues was hanging so low we had to tie them to our belts to keep from treading on them.

"I mean, we tromped through that brush for hours. I lost my hat, tore my clothes, scraped my shins in forty places, and still we didn't catch up to that sucker.

"But finally, just before dark, I bogart over the top of one ridge and just happen to glance off to my right, and there he is, not ten feet from me, grazing alongside a fallen log. I keep real quiet and motion over to the guide and Hammer to stay put. If this bighorn sees me, he's gone, and I figure the only reason he hasn't heard me coming is because he's so old that his ears are plugged with mites. Real slow, I start to train that gun on him until the soft meat next to his ribs is plum in my sights. I mean, that ram is dead to rights. I've brought down men with clean shots at many times that distance.

"But all of a sudden, something happens to me that I can't explain. My trigger finger starts twitching like there's no tomorrow, and so's the hand trying to point the barrel. I looked at that beautiful, one-chance-in-a-lifetime ram, and I couldn't squeeze the trigger.

"The only way I could explain it to you, Boudin, is that I felt that bringing down that animal would have been like shooting into the purtiest picture ever painted or the nicest sculpture ever made. That ram was a work of art, and I couldn't shoot it. I mean, I don't consider myself someone who gets buck fever. If I was starving, I would have plugged that old sheep and ate him without a second thought. If it had been a skip with his gun trained on my belly, I would have taken out his eye right there. But what I did was set down that gun and just watch that ram saunter off toward the tall timber, and I didn't raise a finger. And you know, I turned to that guide, and he was smiling, and I looked at Hammer, and he was, too. They understood, somehow, and I've never regretted holding that shot."

There was deep silence from the other four men gathered around the empty crockpot and the cooling rocks. Finally, Foster opened his mouth.

"Hey, Tiny," he said. "I understand perfectly why you didn't shoot. If you'd have hit him, you would have been stuck carrying out his horns and about a hundred pounds of meat. Ain't no way a fat man like you is going to tie himself down with a chore like that."

The others delivered deep masculine chuckles as Tiny rushed over to the fire to grab the pot, ready to heave it.

"Foster! You son of a bitch!" Tiny shouted as the writer made fast tracks toward the protection of the motor home. "I'm gonna do what your momma should have done. I'm going to abort you at the tender age of thirty-four."

But no sooner did the big man take a half dozen steps than a bullet rang out and ricocheted off the iron pot in Tiny's hand. A second bullet slammed home into Foster's ever-present batting helmet, creasing his scalp and sending him diving into the bushes. Armed with only a small derringer that he carried more for ornamentation than use, Foster thought longingly of the Browning he had left inside the motor home, about twenty feet away.

But after the first two shots, which sent Tiny and the others hitting the turf on full bellies, no others came. After five minutes Tiny made his way toward Foster and the motor home.

Reaching the writer, Tiny scornfully took note of the derringer. "That pepperbox of yours is sure some lethal weapon," the bounty hunter said. "It'll kill a man just like that!"

"It will?" Foster asked incredulously.

"Yep, point that gun at your average killer," sniffed

Tiny, "and he'll more than likely laugh himself to death!"

Foster gave Tiny a rueful look as he picked up his punctured helmet and clapped it back onto his head. The bounty hunters inched toward the Wolfmobile, with Sidney held straining on a leash by Hammer, but soon it was apparent that whoever had been shooting had decided to leave.

Tiny moved suspiciously over to the Wolfmobile and took a stunned look at the windshield. "We've been left a calling card," he said. "Five of them, in fact."

The others hurried over to take a look. There, dangling from the windshield, were five voodoo dolls. One was a likeness of Tiny, similar to the one he had found in the New Orleans apartment the day of the attack on Foster. The other dolls resembled the writer, Jerry, Hammer, and Boudin.

Boudin took down the one made in his likeness and peered at it critically. "Sure hope you boys aren't superstitious about voodoo," he said.

Foster shook his head to indicate that he was not.

"That's good," said Boudin, "because I've lived here my whole life, and it about scares the life out of me."

Chapter Twenty

Sissy's defiance crumbled like week-old cake under the Jaguar's threats. The girl had to reach hard for composure lest she burst into tears, quite possibly with fatal results.

Fortunately, Blinky and Jax picked that moment to open their big mouths. So great was Sissy's hatred for the two lowlifes that their words dissipated her fear momentarily.

"Honest, Boss," Blinky was muttering, "we ain't never laid a glove on her."

"Fucking bitch is lying," Jax echoed.

"I'll show you who's lying," Sissy cried, turning savagely back to Revon. "Both these men attacked me in the most revolting and disgusting way!" she announced. "Neither of them has had time to wash. If you'll take a whiff of their face hair, you'll find evidence enough, I trust. And as for Mickey here, she forced me to do to her what these men had done to me. Her 'juices,' as she calls them, should still be quite apparent on my breath."

Once again the three guilty parties began chattering all at once.

"Silence, I say!" roared the Jaguar, his wrath serving to further agitate the restless cats. "Talese!" he barked at another of his scruffy lieutenants. "Check the lip hairs on Jax and Blinky."

Talese, a rapidly balding giant with bad teeth, yanked back Blinky's head first and then Jax's, burying his own face in their faces.

"Well?" Revon asked impatiently.

"They been eating pussy, Boss," Talese mumbled. "Ain't no doubts about it."

The Jaguar nodded to Talese, and there occurred a series of events so rapid that Sissy later wasn't certain whether she'd experienced a nightmare or reality. The bald giant kicked the two transgressors forward, spilling them to their knees, while simultaneously Revon unleashed the two jaguars.

With hideous cries, Jax and the scruffy Blinky disappeared in a whirl of fur and fangs. Sissy, a few feet from both, watched spellbound as their blood began to spurt.

"And as for you, Mickey," Revon continued over the noise of the rampaging beasts, "let this be a lesson. There will *not* be a second chance. Your guilt is clearly written on your face."

"Yes, Boss," Mickey whispered, her throat dry and fear etched across her patrician features as she watched the two men being devoured.

"What about me?" asked Sissy, anxiously awaiting her fate.

"You?" Revon yawned. "You bore me. I only wanted you because you were a virgin. Pretty girls who've been used are a dime a dozen."

Fearing that the Jaguar was planning on throwing her to the beasts, Sissy cautiously voiced one last question. "What is it you plan to do with me now that I'm worthless, as you say?"

"Oh, we'll get some use out of you, don't worry," Revon replied, rising from his throne. "Mickey!" he barked.

"Yes, Boss?"

"Take her to Yesca. You're in charge of getting her to Yesca." Revon commanded, moving out of the room. "Tell him he can have her as a little present; payment in advance."

"Yes, Boss," the lackey said, taking hold of Sissy's arm to steer her away.

"Who is Yesca?" Sissy asked timidly. "And what does he do?"

"Yesca runs a voodoo cult that's about the biggest in Louisiana," said Mickey, studiously keeping her eyes off of Sissy's breasts lest she accuse her of anything that might incur Revon's wrath.

"I see," Sissy said. "Revon said I was to be repayment in advance for some future favor. Do you know what he was referring to?"

"Sure," she said. A grin across her ugly mug showed her glee at being part of Revon's inner circle. "Yesca has been selected to kill Revon's meddling father and four other men."

"Oh," Sissy said. A disturbing thought formed in her head. "Any idea who the four men are?"

"Your Uncle Tiny, for one. And his three men, too. They ain't got a chance against Yesca's spells. I wouldn't want that man mad at me for all the black gold in Louisiana. They say that just knowing Yesca is after you is enough to cause your hair to turn white overnight. Many's the man who's found a voodoo doll in his bed and keeled over on the spot from a heart attack."

Sissy listened with a deep sense of dread. "And what," she stammered, "do you think he'll do with me?"

"I don't think," Mickey answered, grinning, "I *know!* He's going to use you in one of his ceremonies. With all that blond hair and light skin of yours, you can bet you'll drive Yesca right up a wall."

"What will happen?"

Mickey swept her eyes across Sissy's sexy frame. "I imagine that he's going to fuck you first himself, and then I bet he'll throw you to his followers for their pleasure afterwards."

Chapter Twenty-one

Back in Los Angeles, inside his fashionable Sunset Strip offices, bail bondsman Joey Hudson was chafing as he pored over a file labeled "The Jaguar," which Maggie, his sweet-lunged girl Friday, had laboriously prepared for him.

Maggie fit well into Joey's offices, which were every bit as ostentatious as the man himself. The place was filled with possessions, all of which had some connection to the name "Hudson." There were pictures of the scenic New York river by that name, eighteenth-century lithographs of the famed Hudson's Bay Trading Company, and Joey's prized possession, an antique Hudson Terraplane automobile that gleamed under many coats of navy-blue paint.

For a man who liked pomp and show, Joey's personal life was anything but wild. A Mormon by religion, he did not drink, smoke, chew, or fuck around. But despite all these negative characteristics, Joey was beloved by Tiny and his sidekicks, who swore they'd go to hell or deeper for him. Joey's word was always good, and he needed no legal document to hold him to an agreement once he entered into it. Whether it was a promise made to cohorts high up in Washington politics, to his employees, or to a lowlife hype he'd just bailed out of jail, Joey Hudson was a man to be trusted.

At this moment, Joey was anything but a picture of calm. Not only had he just received a phone call from his wife, informing him that she'd just run out of gas on the Santa Monica Freeway, but the reports Maggie had dug up on the Jaguar were genuinely disturbing.

"I mean, isn't there any crime that this Revon Crozat hasn't pulled off?"

"Afraid not, Boss," Maggie said, folding her arms just below the sweet lungs that stretched her green turtleneck. "He's involved in every illegal scam in Louisiana. In some parishes he's even got the cops bribed or blackmailed into letting his operation work unimpeded.

"What worries me is this army he's got working for him. He's got professional trappers and poachers smuggling dope through the swamps, fishermen and oyster gatherers taking loads back and forth to the twenty-four-mile limit, God knows how many good old boys who'd cut your throat just to hear you screech, and pimps spread coast to coast."

"Not to mention," Maggie added, "the crazies he has working for him, who are into all this voodoo witchcraft mumbo jumbo!"

"Are they all blacks?"

"Not by a long shot," Maggie informed him, shuffling through the file to show her boss a particular piece of research. "My source says that even a couple of wealthier New Orleans women get their jollies by attending bizarre rituals run by a man named Yesca."

"What's so bizarre about them?"

"Strange sexual goings on, orgies, naked dances, a ritual where followers are encouraged to mutilate themselves with razors as if it were some pagan African rite."

"Good grief!" Joey shuddered. "I've got to get hold of Tiny. He's got to know what to expect. Make two calls, will you, dear?"

"One to Tiny in the motor home, I presume?" Maggie asked. "And the other?"

"Get me my mechanic on the line," Joey sighed. "Tell him that my wife has broken down again and for him to send a gas can PDQ."

"PDQ?"

"Pretty damn quick," Joey explained. "Knowing her temper, she's probably kicked in all the doors on a $40,000 Citroën already!"

Chapter Twenty-two

Like the big cat he owed his nickname to, the Jaguar stalked angrily out of the room after his confrontation with Sissy. What bothered him more than losing a fling with a sexually inexperienced girl was the disloyalty of his troops. He figured that fear and money make the world revolve, and it always bothered him when either one failed to bring results.

"I don't understand it," Revon said to a bearded man in his early forties who sat playing a game of solitaire on the plantation home's long oaken dining room table. "I fed those scumbags, picked them up right off the streets, and gave them anything they needed. And all they give me in return is shit. How do you figure it, Captain Carlos?"

A Spaniard bearing a long red scar that crossed his left cheek like a ravine paused with the queen of spades in his hand. "In my whole life I've met but five reliable men," said Carlos. "Two of them are in this room, *mi amigo.*"

"And the others?" the Jaguar asked.

"Dead!" Carlos announced. "I killed each and every one. All were men who swore to kill me if given the chance. They followed me relentlessly around the globe, awaiting their opportunity. Unfortunately for those three"—he grinned, his gold teeth failing to soften his features a whit—"I never gave them that opportunity."

The two men shared a laugh.

"You have something on your mind, Revon?" Carlos asked. "Your brows are threatening to meet in the middle."

"You *are* perceptive, Captain. It is probably a matter of small consequence."

"Out with it, then, and make it even more insignificant."

"By chance," Revon began, "we picked up a girl for our business in Missouri who happens to have a bounty hunter for an uncle. He's sworn to come after her, and my sources tell me that he's on our trail."

"A bounty hunter?" Carlos frowned. "I only know of two or three such men. This one isn't a huge motherfucker with a big beard and a black hat, by any chance?"

"You've named him," the Jaguar concurred. "Man by the name of Tiny Ryder; works mainly for a bail bondsman named Joey Hudson."

"Yes, we're well acquainted."

"How do you know him?"

Carlos pushed down on his long moustache with his right thumb and forefinger. "A long story, perhaps better left untold."

"Come on, Captain!" Revon said, irritation showing in his voice. "Make the tale short but spill it. I need to know what I'm dealing with in this guy."

"There was a woman," Captain Carlos began, "as always there is a woman. This was one I fancied myself in love with, and she died before I ever had time to feel otherwise."

"I take it that this Ryder creep had something to do with her death."

"Correct. Ida was in Beverly Hills, shopping with a sister of hers who had jumped bail on Hudson: something to do with a little matter of rolling a drunk banker who had a thing for being tied up and shit upon. At any rate, the two were getting into their convertible, which was parked on a side street, when Ryder and this big ape they call Hammer moved in for a bust."

"I take it Ida resisted?"

"Yes, foolishly she drew a gun and fired. Even more foolishly, the aim was off, and the bullet missed both men and struck some fag putting up a window display."

"Did they shoot her?"

"Both men did. I claimed the body. There were two bullets in her heart nestled not a quarter inch from each other. This was three years ago."

"So you seek revenge?"

"No, I'm too jaded for those baser actions. I hate stupidity in all forms, and Ida had no business drawing against two pros. However, should they get in my way now," said Carlos, a menacing catch in his voice. "I will take the greatest pleasure in dropping those bastards where they stand."

"You may have to do just that," Revon said. "I've asked Yesca to work his old black magic against Ryder and his cronies. He assures me that his people are nearly ready to do them all in."

"They'd better," Carlos growled. "There's too much at stake in this next shipment were sending out."

"This one is worth $3 million to us, my friend."

Carlos produced a white-toothed grin that cut a swath through his beard. "Not a bad day's work, eh?"

"Not bad." Revon smiled. "Not bad at all."

"Bah! You retire? You're in it for the thrills and risk, just as I am."

"Maybe so." Revon smiled. "Oh, one other complication. This Ryder fellow has enlisted the aid of a Cajun trapper to try to get through to me."

"So?"

"The trapper claims to be my father."

"But I thought your father is dead," said Captain Carlos.

"He is," said Revon. "But that is a long story that I'd rather not discuss."

Chapter Twenty-three

Hammer stood guard, and Jerry got the Wolfmobile ready for a sustained drive. Inside Boudin's cabin, Tiny was hunched over a cup of chicory-flavored coffee while the trapper gave him and Foster a quick history lesson in voodoo. A fire blazed in the hearth, and Sidney was stretched out before it, snoring contentedly.

"What I don't understand is why voodoo took such a hold down here in Louisiana," Tiny said. "Why here as opposed to North Dakota, say?"

"Good question, Tiny," Boudin answered, cutting himself a plug of Red Man and passing it to his guests. Only the bounty hunter accepted his offer. "I guess it's because in the blacks and the Cajuns here, you have two peoples that are by nature religious and superstitious. My ancestors, the Acadians, were great believers in sorcery and witchcraft, just as were the early slaves, who came here filled with their African mumbo jumbo customs. I mean, when it comes down to it, what difference is there really between the Catholic regard for the relics of saints and the Africans' homage to pagan idols?"

"Do you really think that shit works?" Tiny asked.

"Let me put it this way," Boudin responded earnestly. "There's more than one way to skin a skunk, and there's more than one way to cause death. Some recipients of a voodoo doll literally curl up and pine away.

119

Others suffer fatal heart attacks out of worry. Still others die mysteriously. Poison is a real favorite."

Tiny frowned into his black coffee and put down his cup at the mention of poison. Boudin caught the movement and laughed. "I see that you're not taking any chances, just in case there might be something to this voodoo 'shit,' as you call it."

Tiny chuckled back. "You caught me, Boudin."

"Hey," said Foster, getting up off a slat-backed chair to peer through a crack in a cobwebbed window. "I think you got company. I think I heard a car pull up."

The trapper checked his watch. "Oh," he said, "it's just the mailwoman. She comes by this time every day."

"Ain't you going to meet her?" Tiny asked.

"What for?" Boudin laughed. "All I get are bills."

Tiny hauled his bones out of a chair, its aged wood creaking sadly under his bulk. "Think I'll go outside anyway and check out your visitor," he said. "Just to make certain he's only delivering mail."

But when the big man opened the door, a bowel-wrenching scream came his way, and he hurtled through the door as if the devil were on his heels instead of Foster, Sidney, and Boudin. The scream was followed by two pistol shots.

A wretched sight greeted the trio when they arrived at the mailbox: Hammer, revolver in hand, and Jerry, huddled over a grandmotherly-looking mailwoman who was stretched out in the front seat of her Buick station wagon.

"What happened to her?" Tiny asked, his gun drawn and ready for action.

While Hammer tended to the woman, Jerry turned grimly to the newcomers. "Take a look in the mailbox," he said.

The three men gazed inside and saw a writhing pulpy mess and a bloody stack of mail. The hair on Sidney's back stood straight up.

"What the fuck is it?" Foster asked.

"A big snake," Jerry explained. "This poor soul opened the box and stuck in her hand. The fuckin' thing bit her on the wrist twice."

Boudin peered closer at the dead snake. "Water mocassin," he pronounced grimly. "We call it a Congo."

"Yeah," Jerry said. "We got them suckers in Missouri, too. Once when I was fishing, I accidentally caught one of those suckers on a line. I went overboard when I saw what I'd done. I didn't come back for my boat for a month, either."

"Well," Tiny said softly, "let's get this old lady to a hospital quick. Then I think we'd better start searching for Boudin's son before he finds us again."

Chapter Twenty-four

Mickey followed Sissy and Talese out of the room after Blinky and Jax's demise. "Give me an hour with her, Talese!" she pleaded. "Here's a hundred-dollar bill. You can go buy yourself a couple of bottles of rotgut, and I'll be through with her when you come back. Afterwards, you can take her to Yesca just like the boss asked you to do."

Talese's piggish eyes settled on the bill, and slowly his huge palm closed on the green like a giant clam clamping down on its prey. He left without saying a word.

"You came this close to getting me killed, you slut!" Mickey hissed at her captive once Talese had departed. "I'm going to give you a beating you'll never forget."

Inside the room, Mickey pushed the luckless girl up against one wall and searched about for a length of rope. "Reach up and grab that light fixture," the older woman commanded.

"Why?" Sissy quivered. "What are you going to do?"

"I'm going to strip you and whip you to a bloody pulp," Mickey explained, "and then I'm going to ship you off to Yesca, who'll finish the job."

Sissy began to reach for the fixture as she had been told, but the days of torment had frayed her nerves to the breaking point. If she simply gave in, this woman or the lieutenant called Yesca would surely kill her.

There was no choice, Sissy decided; and having none, she decided to gamble.

Thus, when Mickey's hands grasped hers atop the ancient brass fixture, Sissy carefully gauged the direction of the woman's chin and came down with a sharply swung elbow. Mickey had been standing on tiptoe to reach the girl's hands, and the blow caught her completely off balance. Sissy felt a painful but satisfying jolt in her elbow as her downward thrust zoomed into Mickey's parted lips, shattering her nicotine-stained teeth.

Anxious to keep the advantage, Sissy clasped both hands together and drove a second smash into her tormentor's face, landing the blow an inch above Mickey's bloody tooth stumps and spreading the woman's once-patrician nose all over her face. Too stunned even to scream, the injured woman fell to her knees, only to receive a flurry of thundering kicks to the chest and neck.

There was no stopping Sissy's fury. She reached for an ancient vase upon a commode and slammed it twice against the side of Mickey's head. The first swing split the woman's head open, and the second shattered the vase, driving a shard deep into Mickey's inner ear.

Sissy had never fought anyone in her life, but she felt possessed as if by some atavistic instinct for survival as she looked around for yet another instrument with which to bludgeon her captor. The girl's eyes settled on the iron poker leaning against the unlit fireplace. After four strides, she was back to batter open Mickey's skull until no life was left. The whole episode took but sixty seconds, and Sissy was left trembling with the thrill of knowing that this evil woman would never hurt anyone again.

Without bothering to check Mickey's pulse, Sissy hurried away from the quivering body to wash the blood from her arms and hands and then to haul down a shirt and jeans from the closet. The girl looked out

the window and saw nobody as she lowered herself
past a set of wooden shutters.

Luck seemed to be with her as Sissy descended to
the soft earth below, which was soggy with a heavy
rain that had fallen steadily the past three hours. Her
hair pasted itself to the side of her head, and the
clothes she'd taken from Mickey's closet stuck to her
body as Sissy ran across the vast lawn toward a nearby
highway.

"Thank God for the rain!" Sissy grunted as she hurried toward freedom. Ten more steps and she'd reach
a grove of trees that would block her from the house.
She turned for a last look at the plantation just before
reaching her objective, and the action saved her life.
Unknown to her, Captain Carlos had stepped outside
en route to his car and had hauled out a rifle from the
trunk. He had just squeezed the trigger as Sissy turned,
and the bullet scraped past her shoulder and buried
itself into the bark of a cottonwood.

Unwilling to stop, despite the fear in her gut caused
by the whine of the bullet and the accompanying rifle
report, Sissy reached safety just as three more bullets
smashed into the grove. Carlos shouted to some employees who'd come outside to follow him as he jumped
into his BMW and started after the escapee.

Her breath totally gone, one sneaker lost, and fear
pulsating in her breast like a living thing, Sissy made
the narrow asphalt Louisiana highway and saw with
relief that a car was headed toward the plantation. Not
giving the driver a chance to get away, she stepped in
front of a Ford station wagon and yanked open the
passenger door as the driver braked to a stop before
her.

Sissy clambered inside quickly, pushing a bag of
liquor out of the way. "Hurry!" she cried, taking a last
fearful look out the window. "I've been kidnapped. Get
me out of here, please."

But to Sissy's horror, the driver failed to accelerate.

She looked anxiously into the man's face. She'd seen that ugly, mashed-in mug before. The man's leering grin now took in her breasts, which showed clearly through the soaked fabric. Frustration totally taking control, Sissy let loose a long, unhappy scream as a strong masculine hand grabbed her shoulder.

In that long look Sissy had a shock of recognition. She had escaped from the plantation only to jump into this station wagon alongside Talese, the Jaguar's henchman.

"Hi, there," Talese growled, his clawlike fingers bruising the girl's skin and the familiar grin fixed on his lips. "So glad you could drop in."

Chapter Twenty-five

You could cut the gloom in the Wolfmobile with a dull butter knife. Everyone sat there glumly in the parking lot of a local sawbones who had been unsuccessful in saving the elderly mail carrier's life.

"I'm sorry, boys," the doctor said. "Her heart gave out. She just wasn't strong enough to carry all that venom. We tried massaging the heart, but it never responded."

When they returned to the motor home, Joey Hudson finally managed to get through on the mobile phone with his dire report on the Jaguar's illegal dealings. "Looks like you've run into a stone wall this time, Tiny," the bondsman said.

"Maybe so," the big man responded, "but even stone walls will crumble if there's a big enough charge beneath 'em. And if that motherfucker has touched one hair on that poor little girl's head, I ain't going to do nothing less than cram a dynamite stick up this Revon's asshole."

Realizing that depression wasn't doing his men any good, Tiny reached into his repertoire of bad jokes to try to cheer them up.

"Did you guys hear the one about the judge who refused to give Mickey Mouse a divorce?" Tiny croaked in a deep baritone.

Realizing that Tiny was attempting to change the mood, Jerry called out in his heartiest voice. "Hell, no," he said. "Why wouldn't he give him one?"

126

"Well, he looks down from his bench at Mickey and says, 'I'm sorry, Mouse, but the law won't let you divorce Minnie just because you say she's a bit crazy.' And old Mickey, he looks up with this hurt expression in his eyes and says, 'I didn't say she's a bit crazy, Your Honor. I want to divorce her on account of she's fucking Goofy!'"

Seeing the shadow of a smile pass over the faces of the others, Jerry Jeffers stood up and spun one of his own jokes. "All right, brothers!" he said, rubbing his hands together. "What's long and green and stinks of pig?" Without waiting for a response, he chortled out the answer: "Kermit the frog!"

"That's pretty fucking poor," said Foster, smiling nevertheless.

"You don't like it, you tell us one better, then," Jerry snorted in mock indignation.

"All right, then," Foster said. He paused for a second to haul a tale out of his memory bank and then started speaking in a rapid-fire delivery. "This couple just got married, and the best man dropped them off at their hotel. 'Too bad,' he leers at them both. 'Guess y'all won't be able to fool around any more.'"

"Well, the couple don't like this at all because they pride themselves on being real fucking liberal, and the husband tells the best man precisely that.

"'Oh yeah?' challenges the best man. 'We'll see how liberal you are. There's one thousand dollars if you let me kiss your wife's tits.' These newlyweds take a look at one another and get to thinking. They need the money, and the thousand will give them a roomful of furniture. 'Done,' says the new hubby. 'Come on up to the honeymoon suite.'

"So they're up there, and the bride shucks her gown. She sits down on the couch in nothing but a pair of lime-green panties, and the best man kneels down in front of her to stick his nose right between her thirty-eights. He keeps it stuck in there for three or four minutes, until the husband starts getting impatient. 'Let's go,' the husband snarls. 'Kiss 'em and pay me the thousand dollars.'

"This old boy slowly pulls out his snout and looks real lovingly at these nipples a half inch from his eyes. 'I'd love to,' he sighs, 'only I can't afford it.'"

A chorus of boos filled the room. "Tell you what, Foster," Tiny hollered. "You can come over here and kiss my ass. I won't even charge you one thousand dollars, neither."

The journalist complained about the lack of appreciation for his talents, while the others chuckled at his discomfiture. Now that the mood had improved once again, it was time to come up with some sort of game plan.

"How about it, Boudin?" Tiny asked. "How would you go about finding this prodigal son of yours?"

Boudin passed a hand through his slicked-back gray hair. "Well, to my way of thinking, we need to go where there are likely to be some loose mouths around, specifically, loose mouths who are tied in some way to Revon's various dealings."

"From what you and Joey tell me, it shouldn't be all that difficult to find a connection. Not when the guy is into drugs, sex, gambling, and politics the way he is," said Tiny. "But where do you plan on finding these loose lips to sink Revon's ships?"

"Someplace where there's booze, girls, or money to loosen a tongue or two," Boudin responded. "There's a tavern called the Bad Penney in Terrebonne Parish, where I think we can find all three."

"The Bad Penney?" Jerry frowned. "Sounds rough."

"It *is* rough," Boudin confirmed. "The furniture there has about the life span of a fruitfly, because it's always broken up in fights."

"What town is this bar located in?" Foster asked, glancing at a map of Louisiana and Mississippi he had hauled out of his back pocket.

"A town called Tabasco—a proper enough name for a violent place—which is located deep in the bayou country. Legend has it the town was founded many years ago by pimps, thieves, whores, and murderers."

"Then what happened?" Foster asked, spellbound.

"Then," Boudin said, sucking contentedly on a dry pipe, "the *bad* element moved in."

The others in the Wolfmobile gave an appreciative chuckle.

"What sort of people live there?" Jerry asked.

"A bunch of Heinz 57's," Boudin replied. "Every breed of human mongrel you can imagine."

"Such as?" Tiny pressed.

"Orientals, Scotch-Irish, blacks, French, Italians and Cajuns."

"What do they do for a living?" Jerry asked.

"Mainly they deal with dried shrimp for their legal trade," Boudin told him. "And they poach, smuggle dope, and gamble for the rest of their income. Some people called Tabasco 'Smack City' a few years back, and the name has stuck. You can always score a little China white and any other form of heroin you can think of there."

"Sounds like a wonderful place," said Tiny, a look of disgust on his face as he motioned to Hammer to start the engine. "Guess it's about time we paid it a visit."

As the engine warmed up, Jerry rubbed longingly at his crotch. "Say!" he said brightly, "if this here Tabasco is Sin City, like you say, there must be a lot of fallen women there maybe, huh?"

"Just two-dollar whores," Boudin said, "all of 'em ugly, most of 'em diseased, and every one of 'em meaner than a root hog sow in heat."

"That don't bother Jerry none," kidded Tiny. "He'll fuck one of your alligators down here if someone will first drain the swamp for him."

Chapter Twenty-six

Clad in a white smock and scrub intern's clothing, Revon was taking a leisurely inspection of his laboratory in a building adjacent to the main plantation structure. One hundred twenty years before, the building had been used as slave quarters; now it served as headquarters for two educated lowlifes who turned an abundance of chemical raw materials into PCP, cocaine, and heroin.

"Are you going to make your deadline, Don?" the Jaguar asked a portly, balding man who was bent over a pile of white crystal.

"But of course," Don replied, a trace of a French accent in his voice. "Won't we, Benedict?"

A tall, youthful-looking man in spectacles nodded his confirmation of the due date. "We've always made it in the past."

"Just make sure you keep making it," Revon responded, a smile on his lips but his eyes cold as hailstones, "and I'll be happy. And if I'm happy, you get rich and stay healthy."

"A terrific system, *non?*" Don replied, his jowls jiggling like gelatin.

Benedict flashed his stout companion a blistering stare and returned to work. Revon walked away from both men with a feeling of revulsion in the pit of his stomach. Don was a fool, Benedict a humorless piece of machinery. The Jaguar knew that he needed both men, but he would throw either one to the big cats upon the slightest provocation.

Suddenly, the door to the lab burst open and Talese marched in, pushing a frightened-looking Sissy before him. The girl's clothing was disheveled, since Talese had allowed himself several healthy feels in the garage before bringing her inside. Recalling the punishment that had befallen Blinky and Jax, the Jaguar's henchman was careful to restrict his hands to the girl's upper torso.

"She was running away, Boss," Talese explained. "Too bad for her she ran into me."

"What the devil?" Revon ejaculated. "I put Mickey in charge of this one. That was Mickey's last fuck-up. She will have to pay the price."

"She already has," Talese said, obviously pleased to be the bearer of unfamiliar tidings to his employer.

"What's that supposed to mean?"

"It means she's dead." The lieutenant leered. "This hellcat here beat her to death with her bare hands."

Revon looked at Sissy with new respect. "So, my little blond jewel, you're a feisty one, heh? Maybe I was too hasty in not making sport with you."

"What do you want me to do with her, Boss?" Talese asked.

"I'm still turning her over to Yesca," the Jaguar insisted, his eyes upon the golden girl instead of his henchman. "But since it's time for my daily exercise right now, I think I'll get a little workout with this one. Take her to my room and prepare her for me."

"Got you, Boss," Talese said, his grin gone now. The man had obviously hoped that his alertness would prompt his boss to give him Sissy as a reward for vigilance. "Whatever you say goes."

"You seem to have a little doubt in your voice, Talese," Revon said, a frightening tone coming into his words that sent Benedict and Don scurrying back to work.

"N-n-no, Boss," Talese stammered, his fear and contrition obviously sincere. "No bouts adout it," he said, jumbling his words in a feeble effort at humor.

"Take her to my room, then," the Jaguar ordered, unappeased. "And if I even suspect you've copped one more feel, I'll cut your cock off and make you feed it to my babies."

"Y-y-yes, sir," Talese stammered as he pushed Sissy ahead of him.

"Don't hurt her," Revon called after him. "At least not until I've made her a present to Yesca."

"Any special position you want her to be in when you get there, Boss?" Talese grinned lewdly, again currying Revon's favor.

Revon softened and grinned back at the man, a look that sent another spasm of fear up Sissy's backbone. "No, nothing special," he said. "Just tie her spread-eagled to the bed, and I'll improvise something."

Talese led the girl away to the Jaguar's bedchamber, a room sparsely furnished despite the opulence elsewhere in the house. A four-poster bed without canopy stood in the center of the room, and there was an antique commode and a refinished rolltop desk. The walls, however, were totally without adornment. Nor were there photos on the commode or desk to indicate that Revon had any human attachments whatsoever. In one corner of the room reposed two large bowls, indicating that on occasion the Jaguar kept one or more of his pets there with him.

"Get on the bed and take off your clothes," Talese ordered, interrupting Sissy's appraisal of the room.

"And what if I don't?" Sissy asked, a trace of her uncle's cocksureness showing through her fear.

"If you don't, I'll do it myself," Talese told her, unsnapping a long black sheath that hung down from his belt and withdrawing a deadly-looking blade with an antler-bone handle. "In fact, I guess I'd probably prefer it that way."

"Stay away," screamed Sissy, quickly tearing at the snaps and buttons on the clothes she'd taken from Mickey. "I'm getting undressed already."

While Sissy pulled off her clothing and huddled under an ancient quilted coverlet in an attempt to keep some modesty, the henchman fumbled in an old seaman's trunk until he found four lengths of rope. The captive took a frightened look at the hemp and shivered despite herself. There was caked brown material on all four lengths of rope. "Are those bloodstains?" Sissy demanded.

"Sure are." Talese grinned. "At times the boss gets a little too rambunctious with his women."

He moved forward and deliberately grabbed hold of the coverlet, wrenching it out of Sissy's hands and tossing it onto the floor. "Spread yourself on the bed, little one. Belly up or down, depending on which side you want fucked first."

The man chuckled at his own little joke, but when Sissy remained huddled with her arms wrapped about her knees, he began to lose patience. "Let's go, I said!" Talese snarled, hauling Sissy across the bed.

With cold efficiency, Talese tied all four of Sissy's limbs to individual posts. "You're cutting off my circulation!" she complained.

"That should be the least of your worries," Talese answered, nevertheless condescending to loosen the ropes slightly.

When he had finished, the Jaguar entered as if on cue and took in Sissy's lithe body with the eye of a slave trader. "I didn't know your titties were so delicious," he said in admiration.

Revon moved to the edge of the bed and began stripping off his clothes, making certain to hang every expensive item on a chair. He looked over at Talese and nodded with his head toward the door. "If I wanted a voyeur, I'd have sent for one," he said. "Take a hike, Talese, preferably in the direction of the nearest gator-infested swamp."

"Sure, Boss," the henchman replied, his eyes once more passing over Sissy's outstretched form as he departed.

When he had gone, Revon pulled out his knife and walked over to each post in turn, slashing at the bonds.

"What are you doing?" Sissy asked.

"I'd prefer for you to relax, my dear," Revon said in a voice dripping with hospitable charm. "I'd prefer a little lovemaking to rape this afternoon." The Jaguar strolled over to the commode and took out a bottle of Pouilly Fuisse, popping out the cork of the half-filled bottle with his hands. He took a long swallow directly from the bottle and afterward handed it to Sissy, who thirstily took two long gulps of wine.

"Hey, not so fast!" Revon insisted. "If you're thirsty, I'll get you some water. I don't want you passing out on me here."

Sissy handed the Jaguar back the bottle, and he looked ruefully at the contents, which now sloshed around below the label. "Guess I'll polish this off," he said.

Revon took a long swallow, wiping at a trickle of fluid that dribbled past his lips. He wiped at it with the side of his hand and looked over at Sissy with an almost boyish expression. "Sometimes I'm such a slob," he said.

Wine quite obviously had a mellowing effect on the man, and Sissy jumped at the opportunity to ask him a few questions. If she could win Revon over, perhaps he would spare her. At least it was worth a try.

"You seem like a man who has a real way with animals," she began, hoping to get Revon's attention onto a topic he obviously knew something about.

"I always have," Revon admitted, seeming to warm up further to Sissy. "In fact, when I was a kid, I preferred animals to people. Even now I can snuff out a man or a woman's life without so much as a passing thought, but one time I had to put one of my injured jaguars to sleep, and I cried like a baby."

"What were you like as a boy?" asked Sissy, more interested in keeping Revon talking than in actually learning about his past history.

"A killer," Revon told her softly.

"As a boy?" Sissy asked, fascinated despite herself. "How old *were* you when you killed your first man?"

"Thirteen."

"Thirteen!"

"Yeah," the Jaguar said softly in his soft melodic voice. "Sometimes I think that things in my life might have been different if I had used my head, but I was in love, and you know how that is."

"What was her name?" Sissy asked. "The woman you were in love with, I mean."

"It wasn't a woman," said Revon, a grim look upon his face. "It was a man—my teacher—who seduced me at twelve years old. It was on account of him that I killed a man."

"Who did you kill?"

"My father."

"Your own father!"

"Yes." Revon nodded. "He caught me in bed with this teacher one Sunday morning. My father was supposed to be out tending his traps, but he came back early. The teacher turned tail when my father entered the house, and I was all alone. My father came at me with a machete, and I had no choice. There was a loaded pistol on the table. I used it."

"What about your mother?"

"She was a New Orleans whore. I guess she's dead now. At least that's what my foster father says, if you can believe him."

"Who is your foster father?"

"My teacher, my lover. His name is Boudin, and he

took over my life. He helped me bury my father's body and made it look like my old man killed himself cleaning a gun. My new father brought me up, fucking me until I wouldn't let him no more and pretending that I was his son by birth. He made up this whole fancy story about my early years, in fact, but it's all a bunch of bullshit. Boudin has been threatening to find me for years, but though he's come close, he's never gotten through to me."

"Why does he want to see you?"

"Because he's grown even more paranoid in recent years. He's afraid that if the cops ever bust me, I'll tie him into the murder of my real father—and the fact is, I probably would do just that. My foster father's worried that his years of teaching in high school and college would go down the river."

"Why don't you just dispose of him?" Sissy asked. "Isn't that what you do with your other enemies?"

"I will if he gets too close," Revon said. "I've already tried once. And now that he's hooked up with your Uncle Tiny and his cohorts, I'm sure I'll have to plug him if he finds this hideout."

"Does my uncle know about Boudin's relationship with you?"

"Of course not. Boudin's a smart fox. He'll let your uncle do all the legwork, and then he'll find some way to get him out of the picture."

"Get him out of the picture?"

"Waste him. Boudin *does* know these swamps. He could kill fifty men out there, and no one would ever be the wiser. Then he'd try some plot to get close to me here so he could bump me off, too." As he spoke these last words, Revon's eyes shifted once again to the blond hair between Sissy's legs, and he felt a familiar hardening in his crotch. He moved toward Sissy and dropped her onto her back.

"But why do you want to fuck me?" Sissy asked. "I thought you had this thing for men?"

"Girl or boy, it doesn't matter," grunted Revon. "I fuck 'em all."

Revon knelt between Sissy's legs and jammed his cock into the girl's blond mound. Since she was not lubricated, the organ hurt her upon penetration and then again when the man's hardness broke her hymen, which had never known a cock before.

The man moved his cock rapidly forward for three or four strokes and then gasped involuntarily as he shot a load into Sissy's bleeding crotch. The entire encounter had taken only ten seconds from entry to orgasm, and the girl had lost that valued prize she had held onto for nearly eighteen years.

"Some lover!" Sissy snorted as the man's shrinking penis slipped from her orifice.

A fist shot out from Revon's side into Sissy's jaw and slammed her into immediate unconsciousness. Blood poured from both her mouth and vagina as she lay inert on the bed.

Without bothering to dress, Revon pushed his body off the bed and hurled open the bedroom door.

"Talese," he yelled. "Talese!"

"On my way, Boss!" cried a voice down the hall.

"I'm through with this one," Revon shouted. "Pack her in a car and get her to Yesca."

Chapter Twenty-seven

"Say, Boudin," Tiny said, looking in confusion at a map of Louisiana. "Tabasco ain't even on this goddamn Rand McNally. It must be a ittie-bittie thing, huh?"

"Yep," Jerry interrupted, "just like Foster's pecker!"

"Don't you start, Jerry," Foster warned him. "In a battle of wits, I hate to attack an unarmed man. Plus, if there's paybacks coming, you always wind up on the losing end."

"Knock it off, you guys," Tiny growled.

But Jerry's pride was hurt, and he continued the battle while Boudin pointed out Tabasco's location to Hammer, who quickly set the vehicle in motion.

"What do you mean, *I* always come out on the losing end?" he snorted. "It's *you* who's always getting burnt when it comes to paybacks."

"In a pig's ass," retorted the writer. "How about that time I was doing a story on you in San Francisco, and you told me to get you laid before you'd talk. Remember?"

"Yeah," the singer said, his smile vanishing. "I remember."

"All right," Tiny said wearily. "Tell us what you did, Foster. I can see you'll bust a gut if you don't."

"All right, since you insist, I'll tell you." He chortled. "We were staying at this posh place called the

Hyatt, but Jerry was too drunk to score even a *dog* that night, much less a fox. So I agree to pimp for him and procure him a girl so I can get the SOB to spill his guts before my deadline hit.

"The only problem is that I know just about as many women in Frisco as Jerry does, which happens to be zero. So I get myself one of those fuck-and-suck rags and pore over the ads. Finally, I find one that seems appropriate for the star here, and I hop on the phone to ask for a special house call by Miss Candy, whose specialty, I assure old Jerry, is going to satisfy the living shit out of him."

"Very funny," Jerry said.

"Don't butt in, Jer," Foster admonished. "I'm telling this one. Anyway, she arrives in ten minutes flat. In San Francisco you can order a fuck faster than you can get a pizza. Jerry disappears into the bedroom with the woman, and thirty seconds later he comes buck naked out into the living room with Miss Candy chasing him with a diaper."

"A diaper?" Tiny growled.

"Yeah!" Jerry interrupted, unable to stay quiet any longer. "This motherfucker can't order me a regular whore the way a normal man would have done. No-o-o-o, not Foster. *He's* got to call up this slophouse that specializes in broads who give *enemas*. I get myself all nice and comfy on the bed, and the next thing I know, this Miss Candy creep is shoving a tube up my rectum."

Foster held his stomach, convulsed by the memory of the incident. "I told you, when it comes to jokes, Foster Foster is the A-1 undisputed champ."

"Oh, yeah?" Jerry prodded. "What you got is a short memory, you putz-nosed pencil pusher! Don't you remember how I paid you back with the Amazing Amazon?"

"Ooof," Foster groaned. "I forgot."

"Who's the Amazing Amazon?" Boudin asked.

"She's this friend of mine in L.A. who is six feet six of the most perfectly proportioned woman in the whole world," explained Jerry. "Tits out to here, a firm ass, legs long as a giraffe's to wrap twice around you, and a pretty face to boot."

"Jesus Christ!" said Tiny. "You've just described my dream girl. What the fuck are you doing giving her to Foster Foster?"

"Hold on, partner." Jerry laughed. "There is a catch."

"There always is," Boudin said.

"A very large catch," Foster continued. "This old girl turned out to be a . . ."

"Whoa!" Jerry interrupted. "It's *my* story this time. Let me tell it."

"For Christ's sake, one of you tell it," Tiny insisted.

When the laughter died down in the motor home, Jerry told his tale. "The Amazing Amazon is the world's greatest snake charmer. She wraps herself up in clothes made exclusively of snakeskin. Her hatband is from a rare adder. She has a watchband made of rattlesnake hide and boots made of cobra. You get the picture, don't you?"

"Sure do," said Tiny.

"Anyhow, Foster follows me on this story from Frisco to Hollyweird, and I set him up with this woman for dinner at Duke's restaurant. Afterwards, Foster went with the Amazon to her home in Malibu, which is like one deep jungle on the inside. There's all sorts of plants and aquariums filled with piranha and terrariums with live snakes all over."

"It's enough to give Dracula the creeps," admitted the writer.

"Anyhow, Foster here thinks better with his cock than his mind as usual and decides to stay the night. They fuck for a while, and then Foster peters out and goes to sleep. The next morning at six he wakes up with a morning boner and rolls over to park it right between these great big humongous tits.

"He's pumping and pumping, and all of a sudden he stops and lets out the most blood-curdling, bone-crumbling screams this old girl's ever heard. This big fat eight-foot boa constrictor had slithered into the bedroom from somewhere and had arched its head above the bed."

"The motherfucker was looking me *dead* in the eye," Foster gasped, shuddering at the recollection. "And you know what this giant woman does? She just slaps this fucking snake alongside its head, and she says, 'Naughty, naughty! You frightened poor Foster!' "

"Wasn't a bad payback, was it, Foster?" Jerry asked smugly.

Foster smiled back weakly. "No, that was one of your better ones, Jeffers."

Tiny smiled and stroked his beard. "Worst thing ever happened to me was a few months back in San Diego. I busted this old boy on a skip for forgery, and he turned out to have this nice-looking old lady who I was sure gave me *that* look as I hauled him out by the cuffs. Anyhows, I take him to his cell and then, under the pretext of returning his personal effects to her, I go back to the house.

"Well, she answers the door in this flimsy black baby-doll nightie that's cut so low her short hairs are peeking out from under it. We get to gabbing, and soon we get to grabbing, and the next thing I know, she's leading me into her bedroom.

"Quicker than shit, I start to peel down that flimsy black thing so's I can hum the 'Wabash Cannonball' on her little pink titties. But all of a sudden, she looks at me and says, 'I gotta let Pepper in the house. He's my dog.' Now, I got no objection to that, so she scurries out to the back door and flings it open to let in this monstrous black mastiff that looks like it routinely gulps down eight cats, a goat, and two prime heifers for breakfast. He looks at me, and I look at him, and then he flops down on the floor to start bombing out the bedroom with the most disgusting farts you can imagine.

"The stench ain't stopping me, though. I'd had a taste of those titties and a sighting of black wool to the south, and there was no stopping me. I lift up those legs and lift her upside down so's I can suck her out like a watermelon. After a spell, she starts moaning and groaning, so I wrap those legs onto my shoulder and start to play bury the bacon with her."

"That's funny," Foster interrupted. "I got this vision of you with your big ass raised in the air."

"Hey! Don't knock it," Tiny growled menacingly. "Anyway, you don't drive a railroad spike with just a tack hammer, do you now, Foster?" Tiny paused to walk over to the Wolfmobile's fridge and pass out Pepsis all around. "So there we are, fucking away, and just when she's about to come, I swear, she lets loose with a yell you could hear from one ocean to the other. That gets me even hotter, and I start to really pour on the coal. All of a sudden something's got a hold of my balls, and I realize it ain't her hand. This fucking mastiff has figured that I'm causing his owner unspeakable pain and has crept up behind me to do something about it. He's got my balls all secure in that big sloppy mouth of his, and my pecker shrank faster than a punctured balloon. I mean, if he takes one chomp, I'm going to talk like Mickey Mouse for the rest of my life."

"What did you do?" Jerry asked, spellbound.

"I did what every red-blooded male would do at that point," Tiny answered. "I sniveled so loud that the beast took pity on me and let go of my privates. Then I locked that motherfucker in the closet, went back to bust a nut, and marched over to Joey Hudson's to collect my money for turning in her old man."

The merriment in the Wolfmobile continued as Hammer took the motor home deeper and deeper into bayou country, past the shacks of poor blacks and white trash. Once, as they passed a heavyset dark woman, she hoisted up her skirt obscenely and gave them a full look at her ample belly, which drooped low enough to obscure her genital area.

"Hey, Mama!" Jerry shouted out the window.

"Come on back, Daddy!" was the reply as the Wolfmobile zapped down the highway out of earshot.

Forty miles from Tabasco, while Tiny rechecked the weapons and Boudin helped Foster prepare two Cornish hens per man and wolf, Jerry Jeffers unpacked his guitar to while away the remainder of the trip.

"Play a funny one," Tiny commanded.

"All right," Jerry said. "This is by a friend of mine named Leon Nelson. It's called 'Flushed You Down the Toilet of My Heart.'"

"Sounds piss-poor," Tiny announced,

"A shitty, pretty ditty, no doubt," Foster echoed.

"The trouble with you two is that you got no soul," Jerry told them before launching into the lyrics.

After he finished, Foster took off his Yankee batting helmet and pressed it against his chest. "My God!" he exclaimed. "The beauty, the passion, the inimitable insight in those words!" The writer wiped aside an imaginary tear.

"Yeah," Jerry agreed, "it do grab you in certain parts, don't it?"

The singer then launched into a soulful paean to miscegenation that went under the unlikely title "You Were Black, Now I Am Blue" and then put away the guitar as the Wolfmobile neared the town of Tabasco.

"What's the population of this burg, anyway?" Tiny asked.

"About 700 lost souls," Boudin told him, "perhaps 699 of them involved in one form of illegal trafficking or another."

"I suppose the local law is in cahoots with all the vermin?" Tiny asked.

"Yep, the chief coke dealer in town is a part-time cop, and the local judge is as crooked as they come."

Hammer pointed to a large brick building in the center of town that once had served as an auction house for slaves. A large wooden sign stretched along the building to separate the bottom floor from the top. In simple black hand-painted letters, the sign announced to outsiders that they had arrived at the infamous Bad Penney.

Hammer parked along the main street. He felt no urge to park in one of the unlit alleys, parking lots, or side streets.

"Well, here goes whatever, boys," Tiny said, strapping a .357 to the side of his leg. "We don't have no certified copy of bond on this one, remember. So if you get busted on a concealed weapons charge now, you're gonna rot in jail for a night."

Sidney got up imploringly and went to the door. "All right, Sidney," Foster said, reading the beast's mind. "I'll take you out for a walk."

"Good idea," Tiny agreed. "Meet us inside the Penney when you're all finished."

Although darkness was just beginning to fall, the saloon already was doing a brisk business. Inside, a long bar lined the room to the left, and a dozen or so tables were just off to the right. Four picnic tables served as booths, and it was there that Tiny chose to seat his men.

A gum-popping waitress, pretty in a fading-rose fashion, approached the group. "Evening, gents, what's your pleasure?" she brayed in a New Jersey accent that contrasted sharply with the southern voice Tiny had expected.

"Do you have any food?" Jerry asked.

"Burgers and fries and cherry pies," the waitress

snapped. "Homemade chicken soup featuring the losers of yesterday's cockfight, if you prefer."

"I think I'll prefer a double burger," Jerry told her, wincing, "with everything on it that won't kill a man."

"Make that a round of burgers all around," said Tiny. "And I'll have four Pepsis right away."

The others ordered short beers to quench their parched throats, and the waitress smilingly bustled off to hand in the order through an open window next to the bar.

The men looked uneasily about the place and drew a ton of stares from all at the bar. Two old codgers, perhaps hoping to score a free drink, nodded pleasantly to the bounty hunters.

"Don't be misled by the way the locals here seem friendly at first," Jerry mumbled. "They're just edging in for a cleaner shot."

Tiny took a look around the room for possible trouble spots. The bartender was a big man, perhaps in his early forties, but the faded tattoos on his arm indicated that his past life hadn't been spent teaching nursery school. Behind the man, several signs on the bar were indications that violence was prone to arrive accidentally. A bulletin board featured a newspaper whose headline blared, "Three Slain in Tabasco Tavern," and a sign listed eight names under the heading "Barred for Life."

"How about that sign?" Tiny asked. "The one that says 'No Dogs or Fitches.' "

"The Fitches are sort of legendary around southern Louisiana," Boudin explained. "They're all inbred to the tenth generation, so they all look alike."

"What *do* they look like?" Jerry asked.

"Big, mean, ugly, and nasty," Boudin told him.

The singer took a calculated look around the table. "Now, don't you go talking about my friend Tiny that way, Boudin."

Tiny looked worriedly at his watch as the waitress

came back with a mountain of food. He gulped down two of his Pepsis and then turned to Hammer. "I wonder what the hell's keeping Foster?" he asked. "Suppose you and I take a quick look-see outside, partner. You two"—he nodded to Boudin and Jerry—"guard the fort till we come back."

Chapter Twenty-eight

Foster was enjoying a stroll through the old but quaint town of Tabasco. Proximity to the Gulf of Mexico gave the air a salty, clean scent, and he liked the sight of nets spread out in nearly every yard. Only a few passersby were outdoors at that time of day, and for a few minutes Foster was able to forget about his purpose for being in Louisiana and simply enjoy the local sights.

After Sidney had done his thing and then kicked two trenches in the sandy soil with his powerful rear legs, Foster swung the wolf's leash back toward the motor home. But when Foster and the beast arrived at the Wolfmobile, Sidney balked suddenly; his hackles raised, and a warning growl sounded from low in his throat.

"Now, don't you give me any shit," Foster admonished the animal. "I know you don't want to go back, but they don't allow wolves inside bars."

With an effort the writer forced Sidney inside the door and then slammed it shut. Immediately the wolf appeared in a side window, his fangs bared and angry-looking.

"What the fuck are you doing, Sidney?" the writer shouted, his fist rolled up in a ball as he shook it at the animal.

Suddenly, from alongside the motor home, footsteps

sounded, and Foster quickly learned the reason for the animal's behavior. Turning quickly, the writer was confronted by three men, all burly carbon copies of each other. With their massive upper torsos and scraggly beards, they looked very much like Bluto in the Popeye cartoons. Inside the Wolfmobile, Sidney was nearly going crazy, knocking coffee cups askew as he threw his body impotently around.

Foster looked at the three men with a sinking feeling in his chest, although long experience on the road had taught him to keep his face impassive. With a quick sideward movement, he tried jabbing his back into the door, hoping to free Sidney, but a hand like a metal claw dug into his collarbone to prevent him.

"Just wanted to introduce ourselves," said the man who had whirled Foster around. "We're the Fitch brothers: Matt, Martin, and Mule."

Despite the danger, Foster's sense of the ridiculous took over. "Really?" he said, taking in the three clones. "I don't see the resemblance."

"Oh, a funny man," said the lead Fitch. "Do we like funny men?"

The others simultaneously shook their heads from left to right. Foster sized up the three blocks of granite, trying to find a weak point where there was none. He knew that he was only seconds away from a bad beating, but he was powerless to stop it.

Suddenly, their footsteps hidden by the furious baying of Sidney, Tiny and Hammer materialized behind the three Fitches.

"You got a problem?" Tiny asked.

"Yeah," the three growled in unison.

"We don't want to hear it," Tiny told them. "Take your problem elsewhere."

"We're the Fitches," the man in the center stated. "We own this town, stranger."

"Yeah," Tiny agreed drily. "I read about you boys

back at the Bad Penney. You're about as welcome as a
fresh case of smallpox from what I can see."

"Since you're spoiling for a fight," the spokes-Fitch
said, "we'll just have to give you one. We'll go by
Louisiana rules."

"What's Louisiana rules?" Foster queried.

The behemoth looked the writer dead in the eye.
"Him that don't get up gets butt-fucked."

Foster's face went white, but he couldn't resist a
comment. "That's a new one on me," he said. "I never
heard of a queer redneck before."

The remark was like slapping a bull with a red shirt.
The man in the center swung from the waist, but
Foster was ready for the blow and ducked under it
easily. Simultaneously, Tiny and Hammer shot forward
their black pointy boots and caught a Fitch apiece just
below the knee. Howling in pain, the two brothers
turned red as meat, throwing punches strong enough to
brain a horse. Tiny and Hammer, however, were too
experienced in street fighting for the roundhouses to do
any damage, and both men delivered short deadly
chops to their off-balance opponents' necks.

Foster, unfortunately, had his back to the Wolfmobile and had no room to maneuver. The center
Fitch managed to catch Foster by the shirt and slam
his forehead into Foster's face. Dazed but game, the
writer brought up a knee into his attacker's thigh,
giving him an instant charley horse. With a cry of pain,
Fitch drove a backhand across Foster's face, knocking
him into the motor home. Again and again, the man
struck home blows to Foster's body, but the writer
refused to go down.

Taking a deep breath as he wiped off a long stream
of blood from a cut over one eye, Foster glared defiantly at the gorilla. "You had enough, motherfucker?"
he asked.

Snarling in disbelief, the Fitch spokesman hurled
himself angrily at Foster, who dropped to the ground,

sending the heavier man over him to land sprawling in the street.

Tiny and Hammer in the meantime had found the other two brothers to have more guts and brawn than skill. Using street-fighting techniques learned in a thousand battles, the partners decimated the Fitches. In one fluid motion, Tiny had whisked off his primer chain belt and was rat-a-tatting the swinging metal over and over into his man's face. Hammer had palmed two sets of metal knuckles over his fingerless black gloves and was tearing grievous chunks of flesh out of an unlucky Fitch's face.

"No fucking fair," Tiny's man cried when the bounty hunter had knocked his dick into the dirt for him. "You can't use those things."

"I see," Tiny roared. "You mean that it was fair for you three grizzlies to gang up on my writer, huh?" Angered by the thought of what they would have done to Foster, the bounty hunter swung his chain one last time and cold-cocked the fallen man.

Hammer, too, was now playing with his Fitch brother. The man, no longer able to see, was swinging blindly, and Hammer was working him over with metal above and boots below. Finally, when Fitch tried one last desperate lunge, Hammer caught him by the ears and sent him headlong into the bumper of the motor home.

Their men dispatched, the two partners went to Foster's aid. The writer was the worse for wear, but he had thrown his own muscular shoulders into the fray, and his opponent now sported the third broken nose of his life.

"You can't do that!" Foster cried as Hammer and Tiny grabbed one arm apiece of the unlucky remaining Fitch.

"Sorry, brother!" Tiny grunted, "we share and share alike." The bounty hunter looked past the suddenly frightened face of the mousetrapped man and grinned. "Ready, Hammer? Let's make a wish."

Two sharp cracks sounded in the darkness, and the Fitch brother instantly had arms that would need casts for two months.

Tiny whirled and looked at the other Fitch brothers, who were just getting up. "Stay where you are," he growled menacingly, "or so help me God, I'll make you give our wolf a blow job when I'm through with you."

Both men raised their hands in defeat.

"Get this sucker out of here to a hospital," Tiny ordered them, "and don't come into town until to-morrow morning. If I see you or smell you, I'm going to personally carve out a fresh asshole for each of you!"

Chapter Twenty-nine

Trussed up and blindfolded, Sissy lay in the back of Talese's station wagon, covered from head to toe by a filthy army sleeping bag. The drive took several hours, and she fell into a fitful sleep as the wagon glided at the speed limit along scenic country roads.

The captive's unconscious thoughts were of her Missouri home and a time that was free from all danger. She was a little girl once again holding onto her big uncle's hand. Tiny was big and strapping at 280 pounds back then, the celebrated local yokel who could whip anyone and anything for money at every county fair from Kansas to Kentucky.

"We're going fishing, little one," her uncle, beardless at that time, was saying as he took her hand to lead her down the road.

"But Uncle," the little girl had protested, "you forgot to bring a fishing pole."

"We're going hillbilly fishing," the burly youth had explained, tapping the gym bag he held in his hand.

Sissy had passed the afternoon eating a picnic lunch and making her uncle a neck chain of wildflowers, which he sheepishly condescended to wear. The day had gone by quickly, and suddenly the sun was an orange fireball on the horizon.

"I don't understand, Uncle," Sissy had said. "It's getting dark, and we haven't caught a single fish."

Tiny had not replied. Instead, he had taken the child by the hand and strolled over to the edge of a Missouri lake, gym bag in hand. The broad-shouldered youth had removed a stick of dynamite, lit it, and held onto it till the last possible second before flinging it far out over the water.

The explosion came while Tiny was huddled atop the girl; the air suddenly was filled with a tremendous roar, followed by a shower of spray, which drenched the two figures.

"Now, little one," Tiny had said. "It's time we go fishing."

Leading her by the hand, he ran along the grassy shore, picking up one stunned fish after another.

"Six, seven, eight," Tiny had counted as he rummaged in the cloth bag. "Looks like we eat well tonight."

Suddenly, Sissy's thoughts dispersed as she felt the rough hands of Talese seize her. Looking about her, she saw that she was in the driveway of a fashionable mansion. Talese quickly wrapped his arms under her legs and neck and then carried her inside the home through the servants' quarters.

A gaunt, extremely black man stood in the entranceway, with a hard-faced woman in her late thirties leaning upon his arm. Both were dressed completely in black satin.

Held helplessly bound in Talese's arms, Sissy felt the blindfold being torn roughly from her eyes, and she looked up to find the eerie-looking couple tearing open her blouse to gaze at her exposed nipples.

"Yes indeed, yes indeed." The black man smiled, his teeth a dazzling white. "She'll do very nicely tonight, very nicely. Put her in the guest room and wait until a guard relieves you, Talese."

"You got it, Yesca. How many people do you expect tonight?"

"You know better than to ask a question like that,"

the matron scolded. "If you want to find out, come see for yourself."

"Someday I will," said Talese, exiting from the servants' quarters to enter the main body of the house. "But tonight I got something else planned."

"What are you up to?" Yesca called.

"There's a big cockfight down in Tabasco tonight," Talese shouted over his shoulder, straining a little under Sissy's weight. "Fact is, I'm gonna have to burn the rubber on that old station wagon of mine to make it on time."

Chapter Thirty

Upon their return to the Bad Penney, after Foster had changed his ruined shirt and bandaged his cut cheek, Tiny caught a definite look of disgust on Jerry's face as he talked to Boudin.

"Something wrong, brother?" Tiny asked Jerry as he sat down.

"No, no. Everything's all right," Jerry said, but his face still looked a little tight around the edges. "Hey, Foster. What the fuck happened to your face?"

"He cut himself tweezing his eyebrows." Tiny grinned, ducking the cold hamburger Foster threw at him. The waitress came up and scolded Tiny and Hammer for missing out on their food.

"It's all right, nurse," Tiny told her. "We'll just feed them to our pet. But if you don't mind, I'd be grateful as hell if you'd bring us all a fresh round of food and drink."

Boudin sat back in his seat and lit a pipe. "I'm curious, Tiny," he said. "Why are you in this crazy business, anyway?"

"For the same reason any man takes a job," the big man replied without hesitation. "I'm in it for the bucks. I'm a thirty-four-year-old juvenile delinquent with no education, and I got to do what I know best, which is rocking and socking." The bounty hunter stopped as the waitress returned to set down drinks all around; he drained a Pepsi in one long swallow.

"I just can't go out and work a steady job. Now, there ain't no one telling me that I've got to get out of bed at seven and stay at work until five o'clock. In a factory or office, even if someone would hire me, which I doubt, you always got somebody over you that wants you to suck their ass, when you'd just as soon druther shove your boot up it. Ninety-nine percent of all citizens are assholes who are always claiming to be something they ain't. What *I* do, I do well. I'm one of the best."

Boudin nodded and ran a hand through his grizzled hair. "But don't people get suspicious when they see a big boy like you come after them?"

"Not at all," Tiny said. "The fact is, I try to make myself as conspicuous as possible. When I walked into this bar, you seen the way heads turned. But these folks just figure that we're a bunch of bikers looking for a good time. Hammer and Jerry look like bikers because once upon a time they was bikers, though Jerry gave it up right quick once he found out he could get paid for guitar pickin'."

"What about Foster?" Boudin asked.

"Yeah, it's true that he don't look like much of a biker in that goofy baseball helmet he's always wearing," Tiny admitted. "But anyone who sees him probably figures he's a want-to-be trying to suck up enough to get into a biker club. I don't worry about it. Usually I spend my time trying to stay as far away from Foster as I can." This last line was said with a wink and a kiss blown toward the writer.

"What makes you so successful?" asked Boudin. "Is it just your brawn?"

"Hell no," Tiny explained. "About ninety percent of the pickups I have don't require no force whatsoever. They just take one look at me, flop onto their backs, and say, 'Cuff me, cuff me!' I try to look as

tough as possible to prevent trouble. I'd just as soon
shine 'em on with a good bluff as bring 'em in after a
fight. I ain't getting younger, and my body aches after
a fight just the same as yours does. And if I can bring
'em in at the point of a gun, so much the better. It's
a hell of a lot easier on my knuckles, for one thing."

"So what you're saying," Boudin continued, moving
his elbows to make room for a new pile of hamburgers,
"is that bounty hunting to you is a business."

"Damn right it's a business," Tiny told him, speaking
through a mouthful of bun and ground meat. "To be
successful, it's all in what you know but also *who* you
know. My boss, Joey Hudson, has got connections that
start in Washington and end all over the globe. And I
personally have got connections on the street that are
worth several hundred thousand dollars a year to me.

"I stay on top of all my connections," Tiny continued, a finger pointed at Boudin for emphasis. "Take
a hype, for example."

"A *what?*"

"A hype," Tiny explained. "You know, a junkie. A
hype can't hide; he's a creature of habit. If you stay in
the area where his supplier is, you'll nail him or which-
ever one of his buddies has got afoul of Joey Hudson.
I know every drug dealer from Orange County to the
Oregon border in my home state of California. Sure,
the law would love for me to open up to them, but if I
do, my business is ruined. I'll take a trip to jail if I
have to, but there's no fucking way I'm going to give
up information on *my* stoolies.

"And let's say I need help from a local bikers' club.
Maybe one of their boys has gone on a skip or something. Well, since I only go after my own in the rarest
of circumstances, I've got to convince that club president to turn his old boy in, whilst I pocket the com-
mission, of course.

"I take the old boy who's president out to a great
restaurant; we have prime ribs and drink all night.

This all goes on my plastic cards and is reimbursed by the bondsman later. I got to be ready to party as heavy as he can, because he definitely don't want to go out partying with no sissy.

"I usually fix us up with a couple of hookers, and we wind up in a classy motel. Everybody gets naked and has a good time. It's just like any other business, they give parties where their clients get free head all the time. It's just the way things are done nowadays."

The big man looked around the room and shoveled the last of the hamburger into his mouth. In the tavern, seated at other picnic tables, groups of men were playing cards.

"They playing poker?" Tiny asked Boudin.

"No," the Cajun responded. "It's a game that is pretty similar. We call it *bourré.*"

Foster was about to ask a question about the card game when a roar from the back of the room grabbed his attention. "What's going on?" he demanded.

"The cockfight is about to start," Boudin explained. "This is why I brought you all here. The game is a favorite with the poachers and trappers who live in the swamp country. It is my hope that someone here will know the whereabouts of my son Revon."

"Cockfighting?" Jerry seemed puzzled. "Ain't that illegal?"

"No," Boudin said, "not in Louisiana it isn't, though it is practically everywhere else. This state is a betting state, and it has several hundred years of gambling tradition behind it. The governor would sooner outlaw football than he would cockfighting."

"All right then," Tiny said, flinging down his cards and slapping his big black hat around his ears, "let's find the cock who kidnapped my niece."

Chapter Thirty-one

The cockfight was held in an old carriage house behind the tavern. Some semblance of order was kept by the presence of two fences through which passed a steady procession of spectators, gamblers, and bird raisers. Tiny looked at the crowd in amazement. A small traffic jam had formed in what had been an empty street but an hour before. The bar's parking lot had filled, and latecomers had to take whatever spaces were available on darkened streets eight to ten blocks away, a condition just right for easy preying by the Fitches and the other lowlifes in Tabasco.

At the gate, Tiny paid the requisite five bucks a head for himself and his men. In the center of the building was a pit lined with crushed sawdust and peanut shells. Later, the birds would fight on this spot; at present, they were being weighed. A judge took each bantam's weight and recorded it in a ledger, also putting the weight on a slip of red cardboard that was given to the creature's handler. To guard against cheating, the bird had to be weighed again before the actual conflict.

Tiny barely gave the weighing-in a glance. He was interested not in the fight but in the people in the crowd, several of whom might have had dealings with the Jaguar.

Boudin entered at Tiny's elbow but soon decided

that it was better to split up. "We've got a better chance of eavesdropping on someone who knows of my son if we're not together," he said.

"Makes sense to me," Tiny agreed.

"I've got a question first, Boudin," said Foster, who was intrigued by the sport.

"Shoot!" Boudin said impatiently.

"How long has cockfighting been going on in this country?"

"It's as old as the Plymouth Rock landing," Boudin responded, again sounding like a teacher.

Boudin was about to turn on his heel and leave when Foster accosted him. "I've got a question about the weight of these birds. How close in weight is one of these cocks to another in a fight? Can they be about a pound or so off?"

"No," Boudin said haughtily, now the aggrieved professor who has just listened to a student make a preposterous statement. "Absolutely no more than a two-ounce spread is tolerated between the fighters. A one-pound advantage on a good fighting cock is the difference between your weight and Hammer's."

"Now I've got a question for all you rumdums," said Tiny. "Are you going to get to work and find something out about my niece, or am I going to kick your asses from here to St. Jo?"

The troops scattered like dandelion fluff, but Tiny called back Jerry Jeffers. "Something going on between you and Boudin?" he asked.

"Why do you say that?"

"Because you're obviously in a black thundercloud of a funk over something, and the professor seems to be seething like a volcano from the inside. That answer your question?"

"Yeah," Jerry said with a tight-lipped smile, "but there's time to discuss the matter later. Boudin's got one eye cocked on us right now."

"Enough said, Jerry," Tiny whispered, clapping his

long-time friend on the back. "You've always been more likely to make a molehill out of a mountain than the other way around. We'll talk later. In the meantime, I'll keep my own peepers ready for a side view of the professor."

Tiny and his men moved about the crowd, ostensibly to pick up tips on a good fighting cock to bet but in reality attuned to more important chance conversations. All told, the crowd wasn't very large for a spectator used to big-time sports, but two hundred people packed into one carriage house seemed almost overpowering, what with the noise and the sweat of many unwashed bodies.

"Don't smell too pretty, do it?" Jerry sniffed as he parted from Tiny to check out a group of toughs sharing a rum bottle near the only rest room in the building. "It stinks like Syria."

"One whiff could curdle milk and disintegrate dentures," the bounty hunter concurred.

Throughout the carriage house, all conversation seemed restricted to the merits of the birds. Some argued for the fighting abilities of Whitehackles, some for Kelsoes, and others for the feisty Bluefaces. The only other conversations seemed limited to alcohol and sex.

"Did you hear what the doctor told an old boy who'd just had his pecker popped by a rattlesnake?" drawled one horse-faced old man to his companion as Foster passed by them.

"No. What did he say?" asked the other.

"Now you got twenty minutes to find out who your friends are," Foster chortled to the two men, unable to resist butting into the conversation.

The old-timers looked at the writer in stony silence. "Who the fuck asked you, son of a bitch?" complained Horseface.

Foster giggled and kept walking. Tiny used to boast that the writer could walk into a crowded room and be the only one left in twenty minutes. "Honest, Foster!" Tiny liked to drawl. "It ain't only *me*. Nobody likes you."

Out in the center pit, a referee reweighed the opening-match combatants and checked the murderous-looking spikes called gaffs that cock raisers use instead of the bird's cartilage-like natural spurs to make each drive more lethal. Unlike natural spurs, which break off and make an instant kill unlikely, gaffs increase the odds of one bird dying in a short period of time.

When both handlers were ready, a signal was given and the two men slapped their birds' bills together three times to rile the creatures before lining them up for the ultimate battle. The crowd was anxious for the contest to begin, and some last-minute bets were offered and called.

Soon the birds were tearing at each other in the ring, and feathers were flying everywhere. One of the gaffs took out a bird's eye immediately, and a small stain of blood appeared within the vacant socket. The fight was unusually short; the fighting birds quite obviously were mismatched. The winner was a veteran of five previous scraps, and his luckless opponent had never fought before.

But Tiny's attention was riveted upon a large bald man with teeth the color of cornsilk who had just walked into the room. Long experience with working both sides of the law forewarned Tiny that this man was something less than an upstanding citizen. Operating strictly on a hunch, Tiny pushed into the crowd to move closer to the man. By the time he arrived, the second cockfight was ready to begin.

Trying to start a conversation somehow, Tiny looked into the ring to pick out the birds already being pushed by their trainers against each other.

"Howdy, stranger." Tiny smiled at the dome-headed newcomer. "Care to place a bet? Five bucks says the

Blueface down there will beat the living birdshit out of the Gray." The bounty hunter exaggerated his natural Missouri twang as much as he dared, hoping that it might be taken for a homeboy drawl.

"Five bucks," the man scoffed. "I wouldn't take out my billfold for five bucks."

"You must have heard me wrong, stranger," responded Tiny, deciding to lie. "What I said I wanted to bet was five *hundred* bucks."

The man turned piggish eyes upon Tiny, took in the bounty hunter's menacing bulk and the cold dark eyes that obviously had seen a lot of living. "Five hundred, you say," the man repeated. He took a careful glance into the ring, hesitating long enough for the fight to begin, and then broke into a smile when the Gray drove the Blueface off its feet during the opening attack.

"You're on." The man grinned, emitting a foul stench from his cracked, begrimed lips. "The Gray is mine."

Tiny smiled back and tried to sound casual as he spoke. "The Gray is yours?" he asked with a slightly puzzled sound in his voice. "I thought the jaguar was yours."

The man jumped back as if shot and then retreated a step before catching himself. His piggish eyes had a menacing look about them, and his mouth had turned downward in a grimace. "What did you say?" he asked.

With the fear that Sissy was either dead or savagely used, Tiny had trouble keeping his voice low. "What did I say?" he growled, bending low. "I said, you big cocksucker, that there's a fucking .357 inside this black boot of mine, and my hand is on the inside, just itching to shoot low and change your gender instantly."

"You wouldn't dare with all these people here." The man grinned.

Tiny looked into the man's eyes, and his hand sprang up hard with an open buck knife, which ripped through the man's shirt. A five-inch rivulet of blood opened in the man's side. "If I have to use this again, it's going straight into your heart. No bluff, asshole. Call or drop out *now!*"

The man nodded, his Adam's apple working from chin to chest.

"What's your name, asshole?" Tiny asked, a little louder now as a great cheer went up from the crowd.

"Talese."

Tiny looked sideways into the center ring as a second cheer mixed with boos filled the air. "Give me your wallet, Talese."

The man looked defensive. "What for?"

The bounty hunter nodded toward the dead bird in the sawdust being trampled on by the victorious handler of the Blueface cock. "You owe me $500, Poopsie." He smiled grimly. "Your bird just bit the dust."

Chapter Thirty-two

Before Tiny reached the door of the carriage house with his prisoner, his comrades had pushed their way through the crowd to join him—all his comrades save one.

"Where's Boudin?" Tiny growled, taking a quick look through the smoky atmosphere.

"Don't know." Jerry shrugged. "I got the feeling he might have booked. I'll tell you a little more about that at the motor home."

With Foster and Hammer up front and Tiny and Jerry in the rear, Talese was sandwiched in tight as they ushered him toward the Wolfmobile. The Jaguar's lieutenant blanched visibly when he spied Sidney crouched on the floor, looking intently into Tiny's face as if begging for the opportunity to tear this man stinking of cat limb from limb.

"Down, Sidney," Tiny commanded, working his nose in distaste. "God damn it, Sid!" he continued, "you shit all over the floor.

"Foster! It's over in the corner," Tiny said. "Would you toss that alley apple out of the home? Jerry, open three or four windows to clear the air."

"Why can't I open the windows and Jerry clean the shit?" Foster muttered.

"Each of us is blessed with his own special talent." Jerry chuckled. "I guess you've found yours, Foster."

Tiny patted the wolf on the head. "It's all right, boy," he said. "From the stench on the outside, it must have been playing hell with you on the *inside!*"

Without being asked, Hammer had shoved Talese into a chair and had handcuffed him tightly in place.

Tiny moved to the refrigerator and passed out soda bottles to each of his men as they grabbed chairs to congregate around Talese.

"You can make this as hard or as easy on yourself as you want," Tiny began. "I want my niece back, and I know *you* know where she's at. After you give me that piece of information, I want you to tell me where the Jaguar's hideout is."

"What if I don't know?"

Tiny took out his buck knife and sighed. Talese began sweating from the top of his bald head.

"All right, you bowling ball," Tiny said, "you just *had* to go push me, didn't you?" The bounty hunter grabbed the man by the ear and snapped the knife open. "You can still hear with one ear, they tell me," he said to Talese, "but you might have trouble hiding that loss without no hair to cover it up."

"What will you do if I tell you? Will you let me go?"

"I'm going to phone the cops to see if there's a warrant out for you someplace. If there is, you're going with them to get you out of our hair. If there ain't, you'll come with us as a hostage when we go after the Jaguar. I can't have you feeling guilty and hopping on the horn to warn him."

"Let me think it over."

"There's nothing to think over," Tiny roared, slapping the man in the face. "I've got a niece that I want back *pronto,* if you get my drift. It's all over for you, cocksucker! Better piss on the fire and call in your dogs before I get bad with you." For good measure, the bounty hunter added another booming blow to the man's other cheek.

"All right, I'll tell you."

"Got a piece of paper ready, Foster?"

"Way ahead of you," came the reply.

Talese gave a New Orleans address.

"What is it?" asked Tiny. "It better not be a massage parlor or a whorehouse that you've been keeping her at!"

"Voodoo," Talese said.

"What do you mean, voodoo?" Tiny rumbled.

"This place belongs to a rich white bitch who gets her jollies watching niggers fuck little white girls in a voodoo ceremony," Talese said. "There's a big meeting there tonight. I think it starts at midnight."

"At the witching hour," Jerry said grimly.

"What are the chances of us storming the place?" Tiny asked.

"I'd tell you otherwise, but you'd probably tear out my liver if one of these boys ended up getting shot," Talese replied.

"I'd tear it out and eat it in front of you," said Tiny.

"Then I guess I'd better warn you that this place is like an armory, there's ammo and guns stored there. If I were you, I'd wait until those bucks got naked. and started slobbering over white poontang before I moved in on 'em."

"That's good to know," Tiny said.

"Hell," Talese told him, "you ought to let me use one of the guns. I wouldn't mind a little nigger hunting tonight."

None of the bounty hunters staring into Talese's eyes so much as cracked a smile.

"Oh, I get it," Talese said. "You boys are a bunch of nigger lovers to top it off. That right?"

"The way I see it," Tiny whispered slowly through his nostrils, "it ain't skin color that makes a man a nigger. In my estimation, you are a fucking nigger—lower than pond scum and twice as worthless. If those blacks have any idea of hurting my niece, I'll gun 'em down where they stand. But that's only because I'm against any man endangering my Sissy, irregardless of race, creed, or religion."

Sidney began giving an inquisitive sniff at the door. "Hold on, Sid," Jerry said. "I'll take you out in a minute."

"What about the Jaguar's location?" Tiny asked.

"He'll throw me to his cats if he finds out I've snitched."

"And I'll sure as shit sic this fucking wolf here on you if you don't," Tiny told him. "So don't try my patience."

"He lives in a huge plantation house."

"What does that mean?" asked the bounty hunter. "Which house?"

"It's called—oh, no!" Talese's eyes grew big as he looked over the top of Tiny's shoulder at a window Jerry had opened to clear the air of Sidney's dump.

"What the fuck?" Tiny asked.

But as the big man started to turn, a roar echoed inside the Wolfmobile, and Talese's head exploded like an oven-burst potato. There was the sound of feet running in the night as Jerry threw open the door. Again a roar sounded, and the singer slammed the door.

"Who the fuck was that?" Foster asked, looking in consternation at the window and then the shattered face of what seconds before had been a living, breathing man.

"Had to be Boudin," Tiny said, shaking his head at the sight of so much gore splattered about the Wolfmobile.

"How do you know?"

"Sidney was sniffing around before," the bounty hunter explained. "Jerry thought he just wanted to go out, but Sidney had gotten a whiff of him. He liked Boudin, and that's why he didn't growl. No stranger could ever have got to that window without Sidney going nuts and tearing up the place."

"You're right," Jerry agreed. "I stopped trusting Boudin a couple of hours ago."

"Why's that?" Tiny asked. "I told you I knew you was brooding tonight."

"Boudin tried something with me tonight," said Jerry, obviously choosing his words with care.

"Tried something?" Foster asked. "What does that mean?"

The bounty hunter looked long and hard into the singer's face. "What Jerry's trying to tell us, if I get his meaning, is that Boudin tried putting the make on him tonight. That right, Jerry?"

"You got it," the singer said wearily. "His wrist is as limp as a eunuch's dick."

Chapter Thirty-three

After Talese had left her off at the New Orleans mansion, Sissy slept for several hours in the guest room. Her sleep was caused as much by depression as exhaustion. She wondered whether her family had taken it for granted that she was dead by now and had abandoned the chase. "No," she said aloud. "Uncle Tiny won't stop until he finds my body, and then God help the Jaguar and all his men."

A huge-eyed black man keeping watch over her smiled in a kindly fashion when Sissy finally awoke. "Guess you must have been beat," he said. "You sad, little gal?"

"You must have been reading my mail."

"Thought so," said the man, displaying two rows of ivory teeth.

"What's going to happen to me next?" Sissy asked.

The man's smile vanished. "Don't want to talk about that," he said, his voice and diction clearly that of a man with some education.

"They're going to kill me, aren't they?"

"I'm not sure," the man said. "They are discussing that possibility. They refer to it as a sacrifice, not murder."

"A sacrifice!" Sissy cried incredulously. "And what do you call it?"

"I call it murder," came the reply, "but there isn't

anything I can do to prevent it. There's too many of them, and they're just too powerful. They've got plenty of guns, and they know how to shoot. Some day, they say they're going to blow New Orleans apart."

"Why are you with these people? You don't seem like one of them."

"My brother is the leader of this cult. His name is Yesca. Basically he has given me two choices: live here to keep an eye on Mrs. LaFarge or die. It's quite a simple decision, really. I don't have enough money to get away from here, and I don't have the moral courage to fight my brother. Hence, I am an unwilling accomplice to his deeds, though accomplice I am."

Sissy nodded as she absorbed this information. "Who is Mrs. LaFarge?" she asked, trying to fit together all the pieces.

"A rich woman with a thing for sucking black cock," the guard said. "She helps Yesca at all the ceremonies. You wouldn't believe how vicious this cunt is—excuse my language."

"After the last few days," Sissy said despondently, "I'm afraid that I can believe anything. In just a few days my life has changed from a dream to a nightmare."

"They tell me your name is Sissy."

"That's right. It's short for Cecilia. My Uncle Tiny named me. What's yours?"

"Benjamin Franklin Kite," he said.

Sissy giggled.

"I know. Everybody laughs. My mother and father had a warped sense of humor." Benjamin looked thoughtful. "You mentioned your Uncle Tiny," he said. "What does he look like? Every guy I've ever known named Tiny has been big as a barn."

"That he is," Sissy said, a twinge of family pride in her voice. She was beginning to regain her sense of humanity in talking to Benjamin. Also, in the back of her mind, she realized that he represented her only chance to escape.

"What's he do?"

"He's a bounty hunter. He tracks people down and brings them back to justice."

"If he's so good," Benjamin asked, "why hasn't he discovered where you are yet?"

"I think it's just a matter of time," Sissy explained. "Just a matter of time. He'll have my boyfriend with him, too; he's a writer."

"What's his name?"

"Foster."

"First or last name?"

"Both." Sissy laughed. "Isn't that strange? Your name is even weirder, though, than Foster Foster's."

"Guess you're right." Benjamin laughed. "Does that complete the search party?"

"No, my uncle's got a partner named Hammer, too. He's also a big guy, looks like a weight lifter, and then there's a singer friend of Tiny's named Jerry Jeffers who usually gets roped in for the ride."

"Sounds like a crew that would be hard to miss," Benjamin decided.

"They would be," Sissy agreed. Suddenly her voice changed, turning soft and placating. "Benjamin?" she cooed.

"Yeah?"

"If you ever run into my uncle and his men," she said, "I mean especially if something awful happens to me tonight, will you tell them the truth?"

"I can't promise you that, Sissy. I'd be going against my brother, and he'd see me dead. Really, I'd like to help you. I've even been wondering whether I could get a message to your uncle, but I'm a coward deep down."

"I understand," Sissy said, looking crestfallen once again.

"I'll tell you what," Benjamin conceded. "Why don't you tell me how to get in touch with this uncle of yours. Maybe something will turn up."

"All right." Sissy brightened. "He works for a bonds-man named Joey Hudson who works in Hollywood."

"Wait a minute," Benjamin said, interrupting her. "Hollywood, California?"

Sissy was about to respond when a flat hand slammed against the door and Yesca marched inside, resplendent in robes of purple and gold, cut away to show his skin-tight black leotards. "My, ain't this cozy?" Yesca said as he entered.

Benjamin hopped off the bed. It was clear that he was in terror of this gaunt black man who shared a last name and family with him.

"You're through in here, Benjamin," Yesca said. "Prepare yourself for the ceremony."

Chapter Thirty-four

Several seconds had elapsed after the shooting and Tiny cautiously opened the door of the Wolfmobile and held Sidney by a chain to let him sniff the air. "Don't look like there's anyone around now, boys," he said.

"Didn't expect him to wait around," Jerry said. "He wanted to close this one's mouth, and that's all there was to it."

"But why wouldn't he want us to find Revon?" Foster asked. "Think he's trying to protect his son for some reason?"

"No," Tiny told him. "My gut feeling is that he's protecting his own ass for some reason. This one's a puzzle to me."

"Well, at least we've got the address where Sissy's at," said Foster, waving the New Orleans address Talese had provided. "Why don't we dump the body and find her?"

"Not so fast, Foster," Tiny said. "We can't just dump this bird; too many people saw us leave with him tonight. We ain't got time for a local investigation. They'd have us cooling our heels for a month before allowing us a phone call."

"That's so," agreed Jerry, "and I ain't got a particular taste for the sow belly and pork parts we'd have to eat in some southern dump of a jail."

"Yeah," Foster agreed. "It's a wonder the cops ain't swarming around us right now. Someone must have heard those two shots."

"Not necessarily," Jerry decided. "My guess is that the local cops are over at the Bad Penney, collecting some sort of percentage or another from the cockfight."

"All right," Tiny interrupted, "enough jawing! I got a plan."

Three sets of eyes turned his way. "Foster, you clean up all the blood."

"Naturally!" The writer grimaced.

"Jerry, you and me will wrap up Talese in a rug. Take the slug out first, though. When we pass one of those abandoned shacks along the road, we'll toss him in and torch the place."

"Got you," Jerry said, a bit grim-faced as he took out his hunting knife from its sheath to do the disagreeable task.

"Let's go, Hammer," Tiny said, turning to the remaining member of the quartet. "Get us to that voodoo ceremony on time. We make one stop for a human barbecue, and that's all."

Chapter Thirty-five

Fifteen miles north of Tabasco, four silent figures stole away from a lonely, roofless cottage. Suddenly, flames shot out everywhere into the night, while simultaneously an engine started up and a large vehicle roared northward along a narrow, two-lane highway.

"Whew," Tiny groaned, flopping down on a back bunk. "I'm glad that grisly job is over."

"Yeah," Foster agreed, walking over to the refrigerator and pulling out a package wrapped in aluminum foil. "I'm starving from all that work. Anybody else want a hamburger?"

Jerry, seated up front alongside Hammer at the wheel, looked at the writer with scarcely concealed distaste. "Good God!" he groaned, watching Foster tear open the foil to expose the raw ground chuck. "You must have a stomach lined with asbestos if you can eat after seeing all that blood tonight."

Foster merely grinned and went back to molding two giant meat patties. Suddenly the mobile phone went off up front, the noise further jangling Jerry's nerves. Hammer, seeing the singer jump, gave one of his rare chuckles.

Trying to cover up his momentary lack of composure, Jerry answered the phone in an unnaturally deep baritone.

"Howdy," he said. "This is Tiny's male secretary."

The singer took in a few words of conversation and then signaled to Tiny. "Get your ass off the bed, Tiny," Jerry called. "It's Joey Hudson on the line."

"What's up?" Tiny asked, swinging his bearlike frame off the bed.

"Joey needs some help," Jerry said, trying to keep a straight face. "He's just been arrested for grabbing the hoe handle of the California governor at a Zen Buddhist convention."

Tiny flashed the singer an incredulous look until it suddenly occurred to him that Jerry was only kidding.

"Howdy, Joey," said Tiny. "You got something for me?"

"Sure do," said a voice on the line. "I've got a tip where Sissy's being held."

"Wouldn't be a Longfellow Street address, would it?" Tiny asked.

"Guess you're a little ahead of me."

"How did you get your tip?" Tiny queried.

"Got a call from a man who says he's a friend of hers. He claims that his brother has her held captive in this New Orleans mansion."

"What's the brother's name?"

"Yesca. He's supposed to be the head of a voodoo cult that's in cahoots with this Jaguar fellow."

"Voodoo!" Tiny said. "I guess he might be the same guy who tried to kill this professor guy we know by putting a snake in his mail. Come to think of it, I wish he had succeeded."

"Come again?"

"That's what *she* said, Boss!" Tiny joked. "Look! I think I'll get back to you a little later with more details, if you don't mind. Just tell me one last thing."

"Shoot!"

"This brother of Yesca's, can we trust him?"

"Hope so," said Joey. "You never know, though. Maybe it's a trap."

"That's just what I was thinking. What's the guy's name?"

"Benjamin Franklin Kite."

"Whew, that sure doesn't sound like no white man I know."

"He isn't."

"All right," Tiny said. "I'll keep an eye out for him. If he can help us—fine. If he's trying to set a trap, I'll plug him quick and set him out like a big piece of cheese for bait."

"Take care, Tiny. Watch your scalp."

"Yeah, you too, Joey. Hey, you know what's the secret to eating bad pussy?"

"Nope."

"Once you get past the smell, you got it licked." Tiny chortled and hung up the phone.

Instantly it rang right back.

"Oh, no! I forgot," Tiny groaned. "You can't tell dirty jokes on the FCC line. That's probably the operator calling to chew us out."

Gingerly, the bounty hunter picked up the phone and answered in his sweetest voice. "This is Pastor Tiny Ryder," he said. "The Lord be with you."

"Go ahead, please," said the operator.

A masculine voice chuckled on the line. "So it's *Pastor* Tiny Ryder, is it?" the speaker asked.

"Yeah, sure is." Tiny laughed, searching his memory bank but unable to place the voice.

"Well, *Pastor,*" the voice said, suddenly turning to bedrock. "This is the Right Reverend Monsignor Revon Crozat on the line."

"The Jaguar?"

"You got it, fat man."

"What do you want, asshole?"

"Just wanted to tell you that I can find you any time I want to, bounty hunter. Can you say the same for me?"

"Hold on, Crozat. I want to . . ." But the phone

clicked off in his hand. Tiny stared at the lifeless plastic and then hurled it impotently away from him, dropping down on the step between Jerry and Hammer with his head held between both hands.

"Never—motherfucking never," he breathed hoarsely, in the sudden stillness of the motor home, "have I in my life ever wanted to kill a man with these bare hands more than right now."

Chapter Thirty-six

The Jaguar leaned back in an antique swivel chair and looked intently into the scarred face of the swarthy man who was sprawled comfortably across an old couch.

"I think I have this Tiny character a bit riled up, Captain Carlos," he said, pushing a desk phone away. "Are you certain we're doing the right thing in stirring him up?"

"Hell, yes, my friend." Carlos smiled. "An angry man is a foolish man. He takes chances he might not take under ordinary circumstances. You'll soon have his *cojones* dangling from your watch chain."

"I hope you're right," Revon murmured, reaching into a vest pocket for a package of cheroots. "Getting bit by a mad dog is hardly a pleasurable experience. I just worry that we may have underestimated this man."

"In any case, it is of little consequence," said Carlos, swinging off the couch to ease his feet into a pair of white deck shoes. "You'll soon be moving your base of operations, anyway. Wait and see; life in Brazil is so much more tranquil than life in this country: gorgeous countryside, servants at your fingertips, a place where money is law! I lived there for a couple of years, you know. I tell you, we are going to be so happy there, *amigo*."

"I don't know, Carlos. One thing is sure, I don't feel very happy today. Call it angst, perhaps."

"Well, I know somebody who is going to be much unhappier than you in just a few minutes."

"Who?"

"This bail bondsman, Joey Hudson, when Tiny Ryder calls him and they figure out that you sweet-talked his secretary into giving you information about Tiny's Wolfmobile."

A broad grin flashed across Revon's handsome features. "That's right," he said. "In fact, you've just given me an idea. Instead of waiting around for this bounty hunter to find me, why don't I make good on our threat?"

"What do you mean?"

"I mean, I grew up in this country, learning to survive on my skill as a trapper."

"So?"

"So," the Jaguar continued, "it's time *I* devised a little trap for this bounty hunter. If he finds this plantation, I want to have a surprise reception ready for him."

"An ambush, you mean?"

"That's right," said Revon, banging his left fist into his right palm. "We'll have that motherfucker join us for dinner. His fat ass will be the main course."

"And after that, my friend," said Captain Carlos gently, not understanding but condoning the Jaguar's frequent outbursts, "we load up the ship with chemicals for our last delivery in New Orleans, and then it is clear sailing all the way to Guanabara Bay in Rio de Janeiro."

"Yes, you're right." Revon laughed, suddenly looking quite youthful again. "Those idiots Don and Benedict should be finished in a few hours, and then I can give those two unctuous assholes their just share of the profits."

"My dear Revon," said Captain Carlos, moving purposely toward the Jaguar to place a comradely hand on the man's shoulder, "are you thinking what I think you are thinking?"

Revon laughed, a cruel desperate sound, quickly joined by Carlos, whose laugh lines merged with the hideous scar across his face. "You'll just have to wait, my friend. You'll just have to wait and see."

Chapter Thirty-seven

Dressed in a skintight black gown with a slit midway to the hollow of her buttocks, Sissy was taken from the guest room by two unsmiling black youths, who also were dressed completely in black, to an immense, high-ceilinged room that was devoid of furniture except for two marble church altars. The floor was covered with a black shag carpet upon which reposed a dozen candles in ornate holders, spread out in a large circle.

Only three people were in the room. Two sturdy black men in their late twenties, dressed in the same costume as the men guarding Sissy, stood watch over a trembling black girl of perhaps eighteen years, who was clad in a clinging gown as white as a bridal dress.

Not daring to speak or resist, Sissy felt the strong arms of her guards pull her toward one of the altars, even as the other two sentries led the young black captive to the second altar. Without molesting her in any way, the two dark men left Sissy fully clothed but fastened her ankles and wrists with thongs to iron rings in the altar top. Vaguely, Sissy wondered what was to happen, but she had no doubts that whatever was planned had occurred on this particular spot many times before.

Turning her head before a black silk kerchief was bound about her mouth, Sissy saw the other girl being tied down in a similar manner. The girl's lovely chokecherry eyes were opened wide, and her lips were parted to reveal well-formed teeth clicking together in utter panic until a white silk gag was thrust into her mouth. The captive was obviously in terror, as if she knew what atrocities her captors had in mind.

For nearly twenty minutes the two girls lay prostrate on the marble slabs, until a procession of dark-robed men and women marched slowly into the room. Every voice was raised in song, a parody of some old-fashioned black spiritual, led by the deep baritone of Yesca at the forefront of the ghostly march.

Yesca was resplendent in a dark gaudy costume of purple and gold. Atop his head was a gold-colored miter, a parody of a hat worn by Catholic archbishops, and in his hand was a scepter, also painted gold but lined with rhinestones and imitation jewels of the cheapest quality.

Were it not for the grim uncertainty facing her, Sissy would have laughed at the shoddy spectacle of the ludicrously costumed Yesca and his flock parading past her. Like Tiny, Sissy was far from religious, and the whole ceremony struck her as incredibly insane. Three or four of the followers carried torches for additional light, and Sissy was able to detect weapons in the sashes of several of the robed processioners.

Perhaps thirty people had crowded into the room. Besides Yesca and the four guards, there were five other black men, ranging in age from about twenty to fifty, and about fifteen black women. The women were all young, many of them comely, and they looked to be anywhere from thirteen to thirty. Sissy could not help but believe that this girl had once sat in a circle to watch a voodoo ceremony. Perhaps she had committed some transgression and now was to be punished.

Not a single white man was present, Sissy saw, and only five white women, including Mrs. LaFarge, the woman she had seen with Yesca when Talese had brought her to the mansion. Sissy looked everywhere but saw no sign of her friend, Benjamin Franklin Kite.

After an indefinite period, the hard-faced woman began to rise and move about in slowly widening circles with a look of wantonness about her face that made it appear nearly radiant. While those in the circle chanted, the woman moved about faster and faster, dancing sensually to the eerie rhythm, seemingly unaware that all eyes in the room were upon her.

But suddenly Mrs. LaFarge stopped in the center of the room, her body quivering, just as all women do in that magic second or two before orgasm. Her gown was soaked beneath her breasts and in the center of her back. All at once, as if the heat of the garment were overcoming her, she let it drop to the floor, where a limber dark arm reached for it to pull it out of her way.

No longer did Mrs. LaFarge seem quite so old or hard-looking as she lifted her hands to two lovely black girls in their early teens. As if knowing what was expected of them, the two rose and immediately abandoned all their clothing, save for a light purple scarf at the neck of each. They danced in and about the members of the circle, pausing with bodies twitching in controlled sexuality to trace their fingers across the outlines of their own shapely inner thighs and shaved pubic regions. Slowly, the two girls moved toward Mrs. LaFarge in the center, the symmetry and beauty of their bodies contrasting darkly with the light, still-shapely figure of the older woman.

While the two girls stood but a foot from each other, all the voices in the room stopped their chant, and Sissy watched in fascination as the two girls moved their budding chests and shaved pubic bones together as they gyrated slowly in an orgiastic dance.

While they thrust and rubbed against each other, Mrs. LaFarge drew out a large black male from the crowd and began to dance in similar fashion with him. As she closed in tight against him, the man suddenly developed a massive erection, which the woman grasped and stroked, all the while keeping her eyes upon his eyes. The sound of forced breathing and the rubbing of flesh upon flesh rose above the soft beating of a drum in the background. Suddenly, the black man began to shudder violently, and a common curse escaped his lips as he began to shoot all over the breasts and stomach of Mrs. LaFarge. Giving a low moan of pleasure, she squeezed at his genitals as if milking them of every drop and then let go to move her hands luxuriously in the viscous fluid, spreading it over her body.

The two girls dropped to the floor, their hands roaming unabashedly over each other's secret regions, fingers plunging into wet forbidden regions, and tongues following hungrily into those same crevices. Seemingly indefatigable, Mrs. LaFarge arose again to lead another black man into the circle. She undressed him slowly, taking care to place his .357 carefully to one side, and then repeated her actions of a few minutes before. This man, too, contained himself as long as he could, but just as his back arched for the shower to come, Mrs. LaFarge dropped to her knees to take his load into her mouth, kneading at the man's distended testicles with her fingers to relieve the pressure there.

When he had finished, the blond woman arose again and moved quickly into the circle. She placed her lips against the lips of a lovely black woman in her early twenties and orally passed on the semen she had just taken. The girl in turn pressed her lovely mouth against that of one of the white women in the room. For the next ten minutes, the action was repeated again and again until every woman present had partaken in the bizarre communion ceremony.

In the meantime, two other black men moved into the center of the circle and separated the two writhing young girls. Without a word, they plunged their stiff members deep within the girls' soaking orifices and rammed away in total physical abandon. Toward the end of their passion, Yesca arose and began to chant in a low, unintelligible voice, which was immediately picked up by all the other members of the cult, save for the twin-backed beasts writhing on the ground.

Also moving purposefully forward was Mrs. La-Farge. In her hands, she had a long needlelike dagger, which she held in a theatrical fashion, much like a Shakespearean actress might play Lady Macbeth. Mrs. LaFarge and Yesca met at the altar of the black girl, who now also was writhing. However, instead of twitching with passion, the girl was struggling violently against the leather straps that bound her, terror clearly showing in her eyes and the muffled sound of her screams escaping from behind the gag.

Sissy watched fascinated as Mrs. LaFarge extended the dagger to Yesca, who held it above his head in sacramental fashion while Mrs. LaFarge tenderly undressed him. The captive saw that Yesca's sexual organ was of amazing length, at least a dozen inches despite its flaccidity—a state that the blond owner of the mansion soon altered with her hands and mouth.

When Yesca was hard, he maneuvered himself onto the thrashing body of the black girl, while Mrs. La-Farge also moved herself onto the altar to restrain the girl's head and upper torso. The black man knelt between the girl's legs and pumped rhythmically into her, his eyes raised aloft at the dagger he was pointing above his head, with the hilt toward heaven and the razor-sharp point toward the girl. Because of his great length, Yesca was never able to plunge completely inside the tiny girl, and the child's eyes quickly grew wet with tears of pain. Suddenly Yesca began to arc his thighs closer, and beads of sweat gathered on his forehead as his passion neared completion.

When he came, it was with a violent animal roar. He

plunged the knife down repeatedly into the tiny body, showering himself and Mrs. LaFarge with geysers of gore. Unable to believe or withstand what she was seeing, Sissy closed her eyes and fell into a swoon, feeling darkness overcome her like a comfortable blanket.

Chapter Thirty-eight

"Sure wish I knew how we were going to take this place," Foster said, peering through binoculars at the mansion where Yesca was taking his followers through their insane rituals.

"We're going to disguise the Wolfmobile as a soul-food truck and drive it right up to deliver a late-night snack of chitlins and collard greens," Jerry explained.

Foster stuck his tongue out at the singer, and even Tiny had to laugh. "About time I seen a smile cross that handsome puss of yours, Tiny," the singer needled. "You must have gotten hungry all this time, chewin' on your liver from Tabasco to New Orleans."

The big man eyed Jerry gravely, and squinted under his broad-brimmed black hat. "Well, brother," he said, "sometimes I just need a couple hours of stewing to calm me down. I'm all right now. I ain't never stayed depressed more than six consecutive hours in my life. I know better than to go off half-cocked. You lower your guard too much that way."

"Hello," said Foster, peering through his binoculars. "I thought all these cars had stopped coming already, but a big black limo just pulled up. The chauffeur just opened up the door. It's two rich bitches in furs getting out."

Tiny took the glasses from the writer. "Yeah," he said. "Most likely two society broads who got doctors or lawyers for husbands and don't know what to do with all their free time and extra money."

"Hell," Jerry said, "they don't have to come down here for their jollies. They can just call on old Jerry any time they want to."

"Sure glad you're in a feisty mood, Jer," Tiny said. "I finally got us a plan figured on how to get Sissy out of there."

"That's good," the singer drawled. "Just sitting here, I was about to start climbing the walls."

"Good. That's exactly what you're gonna do right now."

"Huh?"

"You, brother," Tiny said, his voice dropping down like a quarterback facing a third-and-goal situation, "are the skinniest motherfucker in this outfit, so you're elected."

"Elected to do what?"

"I just got done telling you." The bounty hunter grinned. "You're just about to go climbing the walls." He passed the binoculars to the singer, who took a long hard look.

"Let me see if I can guess," Jerry said. "There's one wall that's chock full of ivy, plants, and shit. You're asking me to scale that mother?"

"Think you can do it?"

"Sure give it a hell of a shot," Jerry said, throwing off his western shirt and kicking off his boots. "I'll go barefoot. These long toes of mine ought to stick pretty easily into the crevices of those old walls, even without the plants. Oh well, my women always did say I was built like a monkey."

"I don't think they was referring to your long toes." Tiny grinned.

"What are the rest of us going to do for backup?" Foster asked.

"Don't be impatient, son."

"Don't call me son, Tiny. God damn it, you're always doing that! Me, you, and Jerry are the same age."

"No problem, son," Tiny agreed amiably. "Don't get hot."

"But what are we going to do?" Foster asked, glancing at his watch. "It's 12:30 already. Those heathen aren't going to stick around forever."

"All right, Foster!" Tiny said. "You take your clothes off and put on some jogging duds."

"Jogging duds?" the writer echoed.

"That's right."

"Are you serious?"

"Serious as a heart attack. You're going to be point man on this one."

"What does that mean?"

"It means you're going into the heart of that fray, Foster. You're going up to the front door of that mansion and ballsing your way inside."

"How?"

"I want you to pose as a jogger. I know your dinged ribs are killing you, but it just can't be helped. Start out from here, huffing and puffing and making yourself obvious. Most definitely, they'll have a guard or two at the front door."

Foster shot the leader an incredulous look. "You want me to just run up to the front door and invite myself inside?" he asked. "They'll kill me on the spot."

"Not if you're a good enough actor," Tiny insisted. "When you get near the house, pretend like you've just got a savage muscle pull, like an Achilles' heel or something, and fall down in the street moaning and crying."

"That ought to be easy for you, Foster," Jerry said sweetly. "That's all you ever do anyway is piss and moan."

Foster shot him a stiff finger and turned back to Tiny. "Where will you and Hammer be all this time?"

"Hammer," said Tiny, turning to the quiet man who

was standing patiently at his side, "I want you to take your ass around all those cars out there to make sure there's no pursuit. Do whatever you feel will work, but be quick about it." Tiny peered again through the binoculars. "There's about twenty cars out there. Think you can polish them off in less than five minutes?"

Hammer looked at Tiny sternly and snapped his thumb and forefinger.

Jerry looked affectionately over at the quiet man. Hammer was unassuming, but he always took care of business, no matter what that business might be. "Why don't you just shut your fucking mouth?" Jerry asked the man in the white T-shirt. "The rest of us can't ever squeeze a word in edgewise."

"How about you, Tiny?" Foster asked.

"Me and Sidney are going to be the rear guard on this one. Since they've made voodoo dolls of us, let's assume that Yesca and his people know what we all look like. But with that Yankee baseball helmet and those whiskers of Foster's he can pass for a college kid or something. They won't know him on sight, at least. It's a little harder for me to disguise this six-foot-six frame of mine."

"So what's your game plan?" Jerry asked.

"You scoot up the wall just as Foster goes into his act," said Tiny. "Hammer will move into the parking lot as soon as Foster touches the stoop. I'll be here at the wheel of the motor home. Exactly five minutes, no more and no less, after Foster drops on the front stoop, I'll slam this motor home right up the driveway. Hammer, by that time, will have done his thing and will join me when I come hurtling out of the Wolfmobile with the heavy artillery and Sidney."

At the mention of his name, the wolf's ears pricked erect.

"Speaking of heavy artillery," said Jerry, "what the hell are we supposed to pack?"

"Not much, I'm afraid," Tiny told him. "You and

Foster will both be in your skivvies. Guess you, Jerry, can take along an Arkansas toothpick and a rod strapped in an ass pack."

"Got you," Jerry said, strapping on his Bowie knife, which nearly reached the tattered edge of the cut-off jeans he had donned for the climb. "Can I use that Browning 9 mm with the Teflon bullets, Foster?"

"I guess so." The writer frowned. "What should I take, Tiny?"

"Nothing obvious," the bounty hunter told him. "Stuff a buck knife in your jock strap."

"About time he had something big and stiff in there," cracked Jerry.

"And tape your bean shooter to the inside top of your batting helmet," Tiny continued, ignoring the musician's banter. Foster rummaged through his foot-locker for his tiny derringer and positioned it carefully inside the protective metal cap. Foster had never shot anyone with the gun. It was his way of extracting payment from magazine editors and publishers who failed to pay on time. On one occasion, he had shot a hole through an electric coffee pot at a well-known men's magazine, which had earned him a night in jail instead of the $1,000 he had come to collect.

While Foster threw on a sleeveless basketball tank top and Hammer rummaged around in a tool box, Tiny dug out three watches from a drawer and synchronized them with the heirloom pocket watch he always carried. The other three men, characteristically, rarely wore timepieces, figuring that time would press whether they watched it or not.

"All right, kiddies," Tiny said. "Put these on. Time starts with Foster; don't forget that. Exactly five minutes from the time he reaches the door, I want every one of us moving forty ways from Sunday. Last chance to pee or ask questions if you got one."

"I do," Hammer said. When Hammer talked, everyone listened intently. "What is the game plan with Sissy? How are we going to take her out?"

"Good thinking, Hammer." Tiny stroked his long beard and reflected for a minute. "When I come busting in with the motor home, I'll be wearing a bulletproof vest. That way, when I find Sissy, I'll be able to wrap the damn thing around her to give her some protection. But if Jerry or Foster gets to where she's at first, I want them to get her out of the way of fire at all costs."

"Do we shoot to kill?" Foster asked.

"No, we shoot to miss." Tiny looked exasperated. "Of course, you shoot to kill, dumbo. They might have some marijuana up there, but otherwise this ain't no tea party. Anyone besides Foster got any questions?"

There were none, and so Tiny checked his watch. "Jerry and Hammer, you're off through the bushes. Foster, give them ninety seconds' lead and then make like a marathon man." The bounty hunter set down a matched pair of semiautomatic AR18's. "There's four of us leaving," he said quietly, "and there ain't *any* of us coming back unless all four plus Sissy come back."

Chapter Thirty-nine

Foster Foster stepped outside the motor home and began running while holding his breath. Red-faced and with his eyes bulging, he neared the mansion of Mrs. LaFarge and immediately went into an Academy Award-winning impression of a jogger suffering either a massive groin tear or a double hernia. He also grimaced from the pain that soared through his injured ribs.

Falling heavily to the street, he looked around for assistance. Unfortunately for the game plan, a long-haired cyclist in full biker regalia happened down the street at that moment and halted to a stop. On the back of his tattered denim vest were the words "Dixie Rebels."

"Hey, man," said the biker sympathetically, "I seen you go down. Want a ride to the doctor's?"

"Hell no!" growled Foster, grimacing in contrived agony and trying to talk himself out of the predicament fast. He knew that since Jerry and Hammer had preceded him, they'd be watching this complication with bated breath from the wings. Moreover, he could imagine Tiny back at the motor home, staring through the binoculars and screaming in rage. "I'm just faking, man!" Foster said to the biker.

"Faking?" the biker growled, his voice suddenly becoming menacing in case Foster proved either a nut job or a con man.

"Yeah," said Foster, thinking fast. "I'm trying to rob this place here, and I'm going to limp to the door so they'll let me in."

"Hey, far out, man." The biker grinned. "More power to you. I'll be on my way!"

"Just one thing," Foster said. "They've probably been watching this whole affair from the house. Could you reach out a hand to help me and then punch me in the side of the face like you were being a real jerk or something?"

"Sure," the biker said.

He showed Foster his gloved hand; when the writer reached for it, the cyclist threw a sidewinder right into his head. Foster flew back onto the street, holding both his jaw and his groin, while the biker streaked away down the street.

"Dirty cocksucker," Foster said to himself as he half crawled and half walked to the mansion door. "He hasn't learned yet how to pull his fucking punches!"

Three steps from the massive front door, complete with a lion's-head brass knocker, Foster jumped back as a low voice came from within.

"Get the fuck out of here."

"But I need help," Foster whimpered. "I've fallen in the street and been attacked."

"Get the fuck out of here, man."

"Would you send a fellow back onto the street who may die on the front lawn?"

"I told you to get out of here!"

The writer paused for a second. It was apparent that no entreaty would get the door open. Recognizing the voice as belonging to a black man, Foster suddenly had an inspiration. "All right, I'm going," he said. "Just shows you what the fuck happens when you give a fucking *nigger* enough money to buy a fucking house."

Bam! The door flew open, and Foster was face to face with two black men. The first stood about six foot five and was built like an ice house. The second man was hidden by the first.

"What did you say, motherfucker?"

Foster groaned but had to keep up the racist language to gain entrance. The second he had reached the front stoop, he knew that Jerry had already begun scaling the side of the building and Hammer had started doing his thing in the parking lot.

"You can suck my white cock," Foster said defiantly, dropping his hand inside his shorts to haul out the buck knife.

The first man was atop Foster in two steps. He had a piece tucked in a shoulder holster, but he never went for it. His intention was to squash the intruder like a bug with his bare hands. In one motion, Foster flicked up the knife just as the giant came atop him. The writer felt his damaged ribs begin to give again underneath his bandages, when finally, all at once, the black man collapsed. Foster dropped the stiff off himself and hauled out his knife, noting with satisfaction that his single blow had managed to find the man's heart.

The writer crouched low, his ribs on fire with pain, and waited for the second black man to come at him. Instead, the sentry did a very strange thing. He giggled and held out his hand.

"Hi," he said in an educated voice. "You must be Foster Foster. I've heard a little about you, and I'm sure your friend Tiny is lurking about someplace, isn't he?"

Foster's head jerked up and down to confirm that the sentry had guessed his identity and that he also was right that Tiny was just about to come down upon the house like a gangbuster. "Who are you?" Foster rasped as he went to retrieve the guard's gun.

"Benjamin Franklin Kite, at your service." The guard bowed. "Come with me, please. I'll lead you to the ceremony."

Chapter Forty

Sissy awoke from a dead faint to find the ceremony in progress. Her gown had been stripped and her head was in the lap of Mrs. LaFarge, who was reaching over the top of her to take the translucent nipple of each breast between her thumb and forefinger. Even as she regained consciousness, Sissy watched Yesca hoist himself onto the altar, a massive erection already upon him, a tribute either to his recovery powers or to the blond captive's beauty.

Her eyes rolling fearfully in their sockets and her mouth straining impotently to force a scream past the restraining gag, Sissy was only dimly aware that she was now the focus of attention. All other forms of orgiastic activity had ceased. Each celebrant was chanting low the lyrics to another indecipherable song and was following the nude body of Yesca intently as he plunged cruelly into Sissy's unprepared groin.

With incomparable horror, Sissy watched the cultist's eyes turn to narrow slits as he pumped relentlessly into her. Stroke upon stroke followed, and as the passion of Yesca increased, Mrs. LaFarge twisted more and more savagely at the girl's nipples. Above the straining man's head, he held aloft the same blade that had destroyed the frail body of the first victim. Nearly split in two with pain and driven insane with terror, Sissy was conscious of praying to whatever god there might be to help the blade find her heart on the first thrust.

When Sissy felt the man's thighs grow tense, she knew that her last moment was upon her. Yesca came with a savage scream, and the victim shut her eyes to accept the inevitable. Her last vision was of a maniacal-looking Mrs. LaFarge crouched above her, lips spread in a predatory grin and traces of spittle running down her jaw. Sissy realized, as the fatal blade descended, that if the fates had decreed that she be consigned to hell, no terrors in the lower world could compare with what she had suffered during her last moments on earth.

Chapter Forty-one

By the time Foster limped onto the front step, his three companions had sprung into activity. Straining mightily, Jerry had begun to scale the side of the wall, poking his bare feet nimbly into each crevice, taking a toehold where none was given. Slowly but with methodical progress, he moved upward, resisting the impulse of gravity.

Across the way in the motor home, Tiny glanced from time to time at his watch but kept most of his attention riveted on the window above the wall where Jerry was attempting his human-fly routine. Should anyone peer below, the high-powered weapon that poked out the side of the Wolfmobile would cross the unlucky creature's eyes.

In the parking lot, Hammer was the first to find a confrontation. The chauffeur for the two befurred women was sitting atop the hood of his car, a pair of binoculars in hand as he stared at the windows of the upper mansion, snatching occasional glimpses of bare flesh.

The chauffeur, a stocky man in his midforties, turned suddenly when he sensed rather than saw Hammer coming upon him in the darkness. Quick as a coiled rattler, the driver dug his hand into his black suit jacket to come up with a loaded .38. But before he could draw aim, his head caved in like a crushed grape, obliterated by one powerful blow of the quiet man's sawed-off sledgehammer.

Peering carefully through the darkness, Hammer ascertained that no one else was in the parking lot; he then set to work. Using an awl he had taken from a tool chest in the motor home, the quiet man ducked furiously under each car he could reach in five minutes, ramming the sharp implement into their gas tanks. By the time his allotted five minutes had expired, Hammer had succeeded in sabotaging every vehicle; a spreading lake of fuel covered the asphalt lot.

Inside the mansion, Benjamin Franklin Kite quietly led Foster to the entrance downstairs, where an armed sentry sat poised at each door, their minds most likely absorbed in what action was taking place upstairs. At one entrance, Foster found it unbelievably easy to dispatch the guard. The man, a café au lait-colored octoroon, jumped in fright as Foster rushed him. The sentry's Luger dropped to the floor, and as he bent to retrieve it, the blade of Foster's buck knife drove deep into his jugular, severing the vital cord instantly.

Grabbing the Luger in one hand and holding the buck knife in the other, Foster followed Benjamin through a well-stocked pantry to the mansion's kitchen entrance, where an athletic-looking sentry peered out through the top half of a Dutch door. Unwilling to fire lest he alert the cultists upstairs, the writer crept carefully upon the unsuspecting guard, gathering himself six yards away for a leap. But while he was in midair, the sentry turned reflexively and Foster's buck knife slammed into the man's bony shoulder, drawing blood but snapping off the hilt. Snarling in fury, the guard tried to level his 30-30 at Foster, but the writer grasped the barrel and turned it away from him. The two men fell to the ground in a fight for possession of the weapon, which Foster quickly began to lose. The sentry was a few pounds heavier than Foster and a good deal stronger. With a savage jolt, the guard managed

at last to rip free the rifle, but before he could aim it,
a second body leaped into the struggle and plunged a
ten-inch steak knife repeatedly into his torso.

Foster watched in fascination as Benjamin lifted the
knife again and again, tears in his eyes and inhuman
growls coming from his throat.

"Benjamin!" the writer gulped, afraid to stop the
mild black man, who had gone berserk with the blade.
"You can stop now."

Benjamin held the knife tightly, looking more like a
fierce aborigine than the bookish man he was, ready to
slam home the weapon again and again if need be. "Is
—is he dead yet?" the defector asked, looking down at
the bloody form at his feet.

"Dead nine times at least," Foster informed him
warily. "Dead enough times to kill any cat." Suddenly
the writer remembered the five-minute time limit and
glanced anxiously at the watch Tiny had made him
wear.

"Fuck! Fifteen seconds more!"

"What does that mean?" Benjamin asked, showing
signs of calm again.

"Never mind now! My buddy Jerry is going to barrel
ass unprotected into that room full of snakes. Take me
upstairs right away!"

Even as he spoke, there was the shriek of heavy
tires stopping outside the kitchen entrance. Foster knew
that Tiny and Sidney would be clambering out of the
motor home, to be met as prearranged by Hammer.

Suddenly, the kitchen door slammed open, and Tiny
hurtled through with Sidney and Hammer hot on his
tracks.

The two bounty hunters carried AR18 weapons.
Tiny had given the silent man an AR18 when Hammer
leaped out of the darkness in front of the Wolfmobile.

"Goddamn it, Foster!" cursed Tiny. "What the fuck
are you still doing down here?"

"I got detained," said Foster.

"Get undetained!" growled Tiny, surging past Foster and Benjamin toward the nearest stairway. Without hesitating, the writer and Yesca's brother were right on the bounty hunter's heels as all hell broke loose a floor above.

Chapter Forty-two

With smiles bright as moonbeams, the chemists Don and Benedict knocked cheerfully on the doors of Revon's den. The Jaguar was intently discussing a matter of importance with Captain Carlos, and he frowned at the disturbance.

"Yes?" Revon growled, the sound of his irritated voice causing the big cat at his feet to snarl ferociously.

"The shipment is complete, Revon," Benedict informed him. "I told you we'd make our deadline."

The Jaguar nodded at the news. "Everything is ready for packing?"

"Absolutely," Don responded. "It can go on immediately."

After the chemists had departed, Revon turned to Captain Carlos with a thin smile on his lips.

"Well, the fools have succeeded," Revon gloated. "We can leave for Brazil in the morning."

"Why wait so long?" Carlos asked. "Why tempt fate? Let us leave immediately. The men can load up the yacht while you prepare any last business, such as that trap you've prepared for Mr. Ryder and his men. We can deliver our shipment to our New Orleans connection at dawn and depart by 7 A.M."

"Yes, I guess you are right. I wonder if he'll ever stumble upon this place?"

"Oh, eventually he will have to find it. Even a moron would." Carlos laughed.

"I hope the trap sucks *him* in and not some party of tourists from Peoria."

"What does it matter?" Carlos inquired. "Both are a menace!"

Revon joined in the laughter and then summoned a servant to his room. "Assemble all hands, employees, and visitors here in fifteen minutes," he ordered, stroking the rump of the big cat at his feet. After the man had left, the Jaguar turned to Carlos. "What would you say to a bit of last-minute sport before we depart?"

"Last-minute sport?" Carlos asked.

"I must pay off Benedict and Don for their labors," Revon replied. "Since we've no further use for them, I figured it might be thoughtful if I sent them away with a little surprise."

Captain Carlos tugged absently at his seaman's cap. "Little surprise?"

"Yes," said Revon, tugging at the fur of the sleeping cat, "a surprise that will tickle them to death."

Chapter Forty-three

Jerry's agility and litheness had carried him up the ivy-covered wall in less than two minutes, and so he was forced to crouch below the edge of a window leading into the ceremony room until five minutes had elapsed. While he was poised there, the Vietnam vet's mind wandered back to twenty similar missions he had performed as a Green Beret ranger. So often had he faced death that Jerry Jeffers always found himself facing the demands of real life with the utmost difficulty, particularly the demands of the music business. "Money talks and bullshit walks" had become his motto, and he had steadfastly refused to take seriously the idiotic demands various entertainers and record company execs had tried to make of him. Having faced the realities of the bitch goddess Death in Vietnam, Jerry found himself unable to tolerate the demands of her sister goddess, Fame. Thus, at least a dozen times in the past four years, the singer-guitarist had found himself with walking papers instead of contracts.

He glanced patiently at his watch and waited as the final seconds ticked off. Slowly and carefully he slid the Browning 9 mm with the armor-piercing bullets onto the window's ledge. Inside, the room had become deathly silent, except for the droning sound of a chant. Jerry wondered what was occurring within.

When five minutes had elapsed, Jerry sprang forward like a coiled rattler and barreled upward through the open window just as a great animallike scream filled the room. The voice was Yesca's at the point of his orgasm, and Jerry's attention was riveted upon the black man just as the cultist began to bring down the deadly knife toward Sissy's exposed breasts.

With his wits about him and his reflexes operating on full charge, Jerry took in the situation at a glance. He pumped a single Teflon-coated bullet at Yesca, blowing the man's head completely off even as the voodoo leader howled in the ecstasy of his orgasm. A second shot took out Mrs. LaFarge, who was kneeling with Sissy's head atop her lap, leaving the blond captive unhurt on the marble slab.

The singer's entrance caught the cultists by surprise, and he picked off three more kneeling figures before racing behind the other marble altar to shield himself from return fire. Like frightened children caught playing a game of which they were ashamed, many of the cultists scattered through the room's two exits. Those leaving by the double-doored main exit quickly regretted their choice.

The first man through, a stocky nude black man with a wide Afro, was knocked back ten feet by a flying gray shape that caught him by the throat. In full fury, Sidney slashed again and again at the man's face, driven mad by the pumping blood.

The others in the exit caught a flurry of gunfire thrown by Tiny, Hammer, Foster, and Benjamin. Bodies stacked up quickly. When the cultists were driven back in panic, they were picked off neatly by Jerry, who had been able to reload.

Some sporadic answering fire came from the remaining men, but for the most part, Tiny's plan worked like a charm. In a matter of thirty or forty seconds, the room was still, and then Tiny flicked on the switch to view incredible mayhem everywhere. Spotting Sissy's nude form on the altar, the big man leaped forward and began to cut furiously at the thongs binding her to the marble slab.

Hammer, however, had other business to finish. He reached into his pocket and turned the selector switch to semiautomatic on the AR18, pumping in a half dozen tracer bullets. The quiet man sprang to the window just as a dozen or so fleeing survivors reached the parking lot, many of them falling down in their panic and sliding along the gasoline-flooded asphalt.

Firing at the pavement, Hammer splashed six shots into the pool of liquid. The tracers, used to light up the south Asian night, more than adequately served the quiet man's deadly purpose. The fuel ignited instantly and engulfed the fleeing cultists and their autos in seconds. As the flames reached each of the punctured gas tanks, blast after blast rocked the night, drowning out the screams. The New Orleans night was a sheet of red as Hammer peered through the window and smiled contentedly at his work.

"Come on, everyone!" Tiny shouted, breaking the quiet man's revery. "Let's get the fuck out of here before the law comes."

The bounty hunter tenderly held the frail body of his niece in his arms; he had covered her with his vest. The girl had awakened as if from a bad dream, and she clutched her uncle's neck tightly with gratitude when she recognized him, sobbing as if her heart might bust.

"Benjamin!" Foster cried, looking around everywhere for Yesca's brother. "Where the hell are you?"

"I'm here," Benjamin cried in terror. The writer turned and saw the black man cowering atop a fireplace mantel. Below him, snapping at his heels, was Sidney.

"Sidney—no!" Tiny cried.

The wolf turned and came back to the bounty hunter's side, wearing an expression which seemed to say, "You never let me have any fun!"

Then Tiny, holding Sissy in his massive arms, led his men out of the room.

Chapter Forty-four

It was a rugged-looking crew that had gathered inside Revon's den for orders. The crewmen, fifteen in all, had served with either the Jaguar or Captain Carlos for several years, and there wasn't a man among them any less ruthless than his superiors.

The Jaguar sat on his throne with four of his big cats at his feet. "I've called you all here to give you orders and a warning," the Jaguar announced. "We leave for Brazil tonight. I want the yacht packed and the engines fired for departure in precisely ninety minutes."

There was a surprised buzzing among the crew.

"Is there any one of you who does not wish to go?" asked Captain Carlos, his voice unusually pleasant-sounding.

There was a pause of perhaps five seconds, and then two hands timidly shot up.

"Benedict? Don?" Revon asked in feigned surprise. "You do not wish to accompany us to Brazil?"

Both men started talking at once, expressing a dozen regretful reasons why they wished to remain behind.

"Silence!" cried the Jaguar, his face now a menacing mask. "I have given you all the message, and now I wish to deliver a warning."

He bent over two chained cats and barked a single word into the ear of each. Simultaneously, Captain Carlos had moved behind the two chemists and was now grasping them firmly by their lab coats. He tossed them ahead of him.

Eyes wide with terror as they realized what was happening, Benedict and Don screamed out apologies. The words, however, died upon their lips as two tawny beasts sprang upon them, rending the chemists to pieces with tooth and claw.

Revon stood in front of the throne and addressed his stalwart fifteen. "I trust this warning is sufficient," he understated.

Chapter Forty-five

Hustling out through the kitchen, Tiny paused in front of the exit to survey his troops. "Where the hell is Benjamin Franklin Kite?" he asked, seeing their company short by one man.

"He'll be right with us," Foster assured him. "He's fetching Sissy some clothes."

The bounty hunter stepped outside and opened the door of the motor home to let in Sidney and then Sissy, who was now able to stand, albeit shakily, under her own power. Suddenly a familiar-sounding musical voice broke the silence.

"Shut that door and reach—all of you!" it said. "Drop your weapons if you know what's good for you."

Reluctantly, Tiny and his three men raised their hands skyward.

"I see the rat has returned," Tiny said. "I was wondering when we'd see you again, Boudin, you pervert."

His hands securely holding a 12-gauge in his arms, Boudin smiled and kicked aside the weapons on the ground. "Yes, I'm back," he said. "Figured I'd let you gentlemen lead me to my son."

"We don't know where he is, asshole!" Tiny insisted truthfully. "Why the hell did you plug Talese before he could rat on his boss?"

Boudin's smile vanished. "It was my mistake," he said. "I was getting Talese into my sights, when I accidentally put too much pressure on the trigger, and it discharged."

Tiny looked at Boudin's 12-gauge, which was pointed directly at the bounty hunter's gut. "Uh, Boudin," he said, "if you're a bit nervous and jerky with weapons lately, you mind pointing that gun at the ground?"

"No problem," Boudin said, lowering the gun so that it pointed at the earth in front of Tiny's feet. "If one of you causes trouble, I could nail you with both barrels before you took a step."

But no sooner did he lower the gun than it exploded, sending a shower of dirt over Tiny. Boudin had been hit full bore in the midsection with a diving tackle by Benjamin Franklin Kite. The Cajun looked a little less confident with five angry men staring him down.

"Good going, Benjamin," Tiny said. "Think I'm going to make you an official bounty hunter."

The black man smiled, showing two rows of white teeth. Then the smile subsided. "Hey!" he said. "Talese once got to gabbing with me and told me where the Jaguar's hideout is located."

"Where is it?" Tiny asked.

"It's called Magnolia Grove Plantation," Benjamin informed him. "It's right on the Mississippi itself, about an hour north of here. It's on the west bank of the Great River Road just north of a town named Central."

"Great!" Tiny said. "We'll stop at a hospital to drop Sissy off, and then we'll pay our respects to Revon Crozat."

"What are you going to do with me?" asked Boudin forlornly.

"Take you with us," Tiny replied. "Maybe we can use you as a shield or something." The bounty hunter paused, listening to the first sounds of sirens blaring in the distance. "Too bad we don't have another car," he said. "We could take Sissy to the hospital and save ourselves a bit of time."

"We do have a car," Hammer informed him. "A limousine."

"What's that?"

"Well, it seemed a shame to blow a new Cadillac to hell, so I just parked one out of the way and took the keys." Hammer grinned, spewing out his quota of words for a decade.

"Great! Me and Foster will take Sissy to the hospital in the limousine. Benjamin can come with us. Jerry and Hammer can take Boudin out to this town called Central and wait for us there. Is there some kind of landmark we can reconnoiter at?" Tiny asked Benjamin.

"Yeah, there's a seafood restaurant named Hymel's. You can't miss it. It's a local landmark."

"Let's go then, boys!" Tiny urged, opening up the Wolfmobile's door. "Those sirens are getting closer. There'll be some tall explaining to do if we're caught out here."

Chapter Forty-six

Born of sturdy Ryder stock, Sissy already had begun to return to good spirits when Foster and Tiny brought her to the Medical Center of New Orleans, where Foster had been treated several days earlier. Rather than grow despondent about the ill treatment that had befallen her, the girl concentrated more on the fact that she was alive and with people who cared for her.

"I'll leave Benjamin here with you in case there's something you need, baby," Tiny said, stuffing a hundred-dollar bill into the black man's hand. "You're in good hands with this man. We'll be back here tomorrow, just as soon as we can."

Before they left, Sissy arose from her emergency ward chair to kiss her uncle and Foster Foster.

Once behind the wheel of the limo, Tiny made great time, arriving at the restaurant a scant five minutes behind the ponderous Wolfmobile.

Just before Tiny ducked out of the Caddie to join Jerry and Hammer, he turned to Foster and shook his bearlike head. "Foster, I got a premonition," he said. "Or you might call it an educated guess."

"What are you thinking?" Foster asked.

"It just seems to me that a man like Revon wouldn't have got where he's got without a little brain matter. I'd bet he's prepared a reception for us."

"You mean a trap?"

"I mean *just* that," Tiny concurred. "My groin's

itching, my pits are throbbing, and I got a stabbing sensation two or three other places that just won't quit."

"Maybe you need a bath," Foster said, hastening to take back his ill-advised joke when Tiny rolled up the sleeves on his shirt.

The bounty hunter's mind was made up when he yanked open the Wolfmobile's door. "Jerry, Hammer! Let's get all our artillery into the back of the limo. Foster, put Sidney in the front seat next to me. All of us are gonna ride in the Caddie."

"What about me?" Boudin asked.

"You're driving the Wolfmobile right up to the front door of the plantation house. I'll be right in back of you. If you try any funny business, I'll blow you away," Tiny said, cuffing Boudin's hands together.

"I can see that you suspect a trap, Tiny," Boudin announced, trying to use his professional powers of persuasion. "But if there is a trap, I'll be killed."

"Yeah, and I'll be alive. Ain't it wonderful?"

With Tiny, Sidney, and Jerry up front sitting under the open moon-roof and Foster teamed up in back with Hammer, the limo pulled out onto the highway, right behind the Wolfmobile.

But Boudin Crozat never was to get a glimpse of the man whose father he had helped kill. Tiny's instincts had saved him once again. As the Wolfmobile drove up the well-shaded driveway leading to the plantation house, the top of the motor home slapped hard into the low-slung boughs of a two-hundred-year-old oak tree, which suddenly exploded with enough force to shatter dozens of windows in Magnolia Grove. The entire cab of the vehicle was blown away, and there wasn't much more left of Boudin than a red strip of meat between the handcuffs.

Ignoring the nearness of death once again, Tiny turned to Jerry and shrugged. "Shit!" the bounty hunter lamented. "That's the third motor home I lost this year."

Chapter Forty-seven

Just before the explosion, Revon and Captain Carlos had led three of the Jaguar's prize cats into cages set in the back of a pickup truck. A fourth cat, a monstrous beast of 240 pounds, was already aboard the luxurious yacht.

"This does it," Carlos announced. "In a short time we'll be in New Orleans to drop off the shipment, and right after that we'll be on the high seas, ready to live the rest of our lives as kings."

"Are you certain your connection will be there?" the Jaguar asked. "How do you know he'll get up?"

"His share of the loot comes to more than a $1 million," the captain insisted. "I think any man would give up a little beauty sleep for that much cash."

But the captain's mirth shut off instantly when the explosion sounded from the long driveway.

"Do you think it's the bounty hunter?" Revon asked.

"This time of night, who else could it be?" responded Carlos. "Let's get out of here!"

The plantation house was only a half mile from the river. Two hundred years before, it had been even closer, but the fickle Mississippi had changed its course. While Tiny and his men sped toward the house from the south, Revon and Carlos headed east toward the ship. After the vehicle had gone several hundred yards, Captain Carlos decided to dust the lights.

"Did you see that?" Foster cried from the passenger seat.

"See what?" Tiny echoed from across the way.

"A car or truck is headed from the house and is going toward the levee," Foster shouted excitedly, causing Sidney beside him to growl anxiously.

"Are you sure?" asked Tiny, whose eyes had been upon the house.

"I'll bet my reputation on it," Foster replied.

Tiny scowled. "That ain't saying much, Foster!"

"All right, Tiny," Foster said stoutly. "I'll bet *yours!*"

"Whew!" Tiny said. "Now you're talking! Maybe there's something to what you're saying."

The bounty hunter gunned the limousine up to eighty, spraying gravel everywhere, as he headed east toward the levee.

But Carlos and Revon had gotten too much of a head start on the limo. As the two fugitives piled out of the pickup, the Jaguar made a move to rush back to free his cats, but Carlos screamed at him to desist.

"You can train more in Brazil. Look at their lights. They'll be here in a second."

The two men raced up the gangplank, with Captain Carlos issuing furious orders in Spanish. The yacht's engines had long since been warmed up, and the boat began immediately to swing out toward the heart of the muddy Mississippi.

By the time Tiny hit the levee top and drove down toward the concrete pier, the boat was fifty feet away. On orders from Captain Carlos, several crew members raced up to the stern and began firing. One bullet hit the windshield and shattered it.

"Why, you motherfuckers!" Tiny cried. "Hold on, boys!" The bounty hunter put his foot down to the accelerator, and the Caddie responded by fairly exploding down the ramp.

"Holy jump-up, sit-down!" Foster cried, closing his eyes as he realized what Tiny was about to do.

In the back seat, Hammer and Jerry braced themselves for the inevitable jolt. The only uncertainty was whether the jolt would come from pitching headlong into the deep, dirty river or from ramming atop or alongside the yacht. The limo seemed to hang forever in midair, and the hearts of the men in the Caddie stood ready to climb out of their throats.

With an ear-splitting shock, the car sailed onto the yacht's broad low stern, taking out a brass rail with its trunk end. The impact blew out three tires and caved in a goodly portion of deck. Dazed but conscious, Tiny and his men threw open the doors and moon-roof, their guns blazing. The bounty hunter and Hammer wielded AR18's while Jerry and Foster handled revolvers, the singer with a Browning and the writer with Tiny's .357.

The odds were fourteen men to four. The enemy's strength had just been reduced by one sharpshooter, who had slipped in the stern while trying unsuccessfully to escape from the descending Cadillac. The limo had driven him into the deck like a fleshy spike.

Another crew member was killed by Sidney, who had had vaulted out the moon-roof upon impact and set his fangs into a Spanish-speaking galley cook better known for his prowess with a stiletto than with a carving knife. Two more were cut in half by the first burst of Tiny's automatic, and another lay bleeding on the deck with a shattered hip.

Seeing his team reduced to nine in a matter of seconds, Revon screamed at his forces to set up behind barricades, while he himself skittered low across the deck to free the last remaining jaguar. The big cat, however, was scared and angry because of the noise and rocking waters. Instead of charging the invaders, the big cat raced toward the other end of the deck, sending two men flying into the raging Mississippi rather than face certain death from evisceration. They bobbed for several seconds, frantically flailing at the churning water in an effort to avoid the boat, and then they were swept under to become food for channel cats.

Up on the bridge, Captain Carlos handed his man at the helm a pistol and leaned out one side of the glass window, firing down at the intruders with a long-barreled .44. One shot splintered through a metal door in the rear of the limo and tore out a chunk of flesh from Jerry's thigh. The singer grabbed his leg and flopped onto the deck, only to be dragged into the car by Hammer, who had dived inside to aid his comrade.

Unable to spot Revon's forces and unwilling to be mowed down by Captain Carlos from his position of advantage, Tiny maneuvered himself inside the car and started it again. Although the engine instantly seized up in a murderous roar, the transmission worked well enough to propel the car out of the divots in the deck.

As the car bucked ahead, Captain Carlos again leaned forward, hoping to score a hit on Tiny's exposed flesh. Instead, the .44 bullet slammed harmlessly into the car's roof and rebounded away. But Tiny's aim was truer. The automatic burped again and again. When it stopped, the helmsman lay draped in death atop the wheel, and Carlos toppled backward from the bridge to lie bleeding but conscious on the deck. While Revon watched from his hiding place behind some cargo, the rampaging big cat trotted up on padded feet to Carlos and began filling itself on the dying man's exposed innards.

Sidney, in the meantime, had added one more enemy soldier to his credit. The boatswain had tried to flee toward an open cabin but had been unable to close the door behind him as the gray wolf hit him with a tornado's force. The man was slammed back into an oak wall and managed to hold on to his pistol for one shot. The bullet tore through Sidney's ear and embedded itself in the body of the first mate, who had rushed over, hoping to pry the wolf off the boatswain. Clamping his powerful jaws about the man's wrist, Sidney chewed through to the marrow and then slashed viciously at the doomed man's throat until the bubble of life broke.

Meanwhile, on the deck, Hammer had also gone down with a bullet, which buried itself high in his chest. Before losing consciousness, the quiet man felt Tiny push him into the back seat of the Caddie, where he lay alongside Jerry, who was holding his gun poised in case the enemy broke past Tiny and Foster.

Within three minutes, the odds had been reduced to six to two in Revon's favor, but two of his men were downstairs, working the engine room. They never succeeded in getting to the fray. Ignoring a barrage of bullets that claimed his batting helmet and tore out some of his whiskers, Foster managed to slide down the stairs to the engine room, where he dispatched both workers in an exchange of fire.

A bearded Latin face appeared in the exit. As in a duel, both Foster and the Latino fired; but though the latter squeezed the trigger first, his gun jammed on him. With a prayer to his Muse and all the stars, Foster pumped a slug into the man's heart.

With the odds now three to two in Revon's favor, Tiny searched the deck, looking for fresh targets, but instead saw two paunchy older men walking toward him with their hands held aloft in surrender. The bounty hunter shouted at them to drop their weapons, which they did, but then both men fell dead upon the deck. Screaming in Cajun at them for their cowardly display, Revon had slaughtered his own men rather than have them captured.

Although he was the only defender left, Revon refused to give up. He still had one ace in the hole in the form of the berserk animal that had given him his nick-name. The animal came close to trumping Tiny forever.

Hurtling forward with his automatic weapon blazing to keep Revon pinned behind the cargo, the bounty hunter looked up to see several hundred pounds of furious cat already completing its leap from the bridge. Tiny tried to change the direction of his fire but knew deep within his bowels that it was too late. But instead of feeling the expected blow against his chest, Tiny felt another body leap over his shoulder.

Seeing Tiny's predicament, Sidney had raced up to throw his body into the big cat's path. The wolf was outweighed, and the cat's leap broke his neck like balsawood. But as Sidney lay dying on the deck, the pause gave Tiny time enough to empty his weapon into the big cat's brain.

Reacting like an enraged animal himself, Tiny stormed toward Revon just as the latter stepped out from behind cover. The Jaguar shot twice, catching Tiny in the fleshy part of the cheek with one bullet but missing completely with the second.

He was never to get a third shot. Tiny hit him broad-side with a swing that broke the man's jaw into ten pieces. When he went down, the streetfighter turned bounty hunter started whaling away with his boots, re-ducing Revon's once-handsome face to a shapeless mass of bleeding protoplasm. He was dead in thirty seconds.

While Tiny stomped the Jaguar to an ignominious pulp, Foster was standing atop the corpse of the helms-man, trying in vain to steer the yacht. Tiny looked up and saw a mothball freighter dead ahead and then shifted his gaze to the bridge for a memorable glimpse of the would-be Captain Ahab standing paralyzed in fear, his hands shut tight over his eyes to blot out the sight of the rusted frame dead ahead.

"Oh, shit—oh, shit!" Foster cried as the prow acci-dentally slammed full force into the giant fighter. The writer leaned out from the bridge and shrugged as the yacht quickly began to fill up with water.

"Uh, Foster," Tiny said sympathetically as the writer walked red-faced down the bridge stairs, "I guess it ain't exactly like steering your pecker in the bathtub, is it?"

Chapter Forty-eight

It took $500, but Tiny managed to bribe a passing houseboater to take his injured men, himself, and Foster aboard and to New Orleans, shortly after daylight. Jerry and Hammer were able to move under their own power and they insisted that Tiny allow them to help place Sidney's broken body into a gunny sack to dispose of it in a watery grave.

Before leaving, Tiny made a ship-to-shore phone call to Joey Hudson in L.A., asking him to pull whatever strings he could to clear the case with the Louisiana authorities. Several million dollars' worth of narcotics might sweeten some moods, although the shipment would be a trifle soggy by the time the lawmen retrieved it.

At the medical center, it was determined that Hammer and Jerry's injuries would keep them under covers for a couple of days. Sissy, however, was ready to be released.

"She'll need lots of loving care," the attending physician warned Tiny and Foster.

"Don't worry," growled Tiny, throwing a tattooed arm around his niece, as if protecting her from the writer. "For the last few days she's been loved nothing but wrong, and I aim to see she gets treated *right*. We'll give her all the family love she can handle. And if she wants a piece of green cheese, I'll damn sure go to the moon and back to bring her a piece."

ABOUT THE AUTHORS

Tiny Boyles is a latterday bounty hunter who roams the U.S. to bring back bail-skips and assorted nogoodniks. His exploits have been chronicled by Tom Snyder, "Speak Up America," "PM Magazine," *Oui*, the *Los Angeles Times* and numerous foreign publications.

Hank Nuwer is an itinerant writer who on assignment has blasted into bad guys' hideouts with bounty hunter Tiny Boyles, flown Idaho's unfriendly skies with backcountry pilots in midwinter, herded with Basque sheepherders, joined ecological saboteurs on their appointed rounds, and played baseball with the Montreal Expos' farm teams. His experiences have been noted in periodicals and on television shows across the country.